Percy Wynn

or, Making a Boy of Him

by

FRANCIS J. FINN, S.J.

Author of "Tom Playfair," "Harry Dee,"
"Claude Lightfoot," etc.

NEW YORK,
BOSTON, CINCINNATI, CHICAGO, SAN FRANCISCO
BENZIGER BROTHERS, INC.

CONTENTS

—·—

Father Francis J. Finn,

(born St. Louis, Missouri, 1859, died Cincinnati, OH, November 2, 1928). was an American Jesuit priest who wrote a series of 27 popular novels for young people. The books contain fun stories, likeable characters and themes that remain current in today's world. Each story conveys an important moral precept.The son of Irish immigrant parents, Francis J. Finn was born on October 4, 1859, in St. Louis, Missouri; there he grew up, attending parochial schools. As a boy, Francis was deeply impressed with Cardinal Wiseman's famous novel of the early Christian martyrs, Fabiola. Eleven-year-old Francis was a voracious reader; he read the works of Charles Dickens, devouring Nicholas Nickleby and The Pickwick Papers. From his First Communion at age 12, Francis began to desire to become a Jesuit priest. Fr. Charles Coppens urged Francis to apply himself to his Latin, to improve it by using an all-Latin prayerbook, and to read good Catholic books. Fr. Finn credited his vocation to this advice and to his membership in the Sodality of Our Lady.He entered the Society of Jesus in 1879 after graduating from St. Louis University. Francis began his Jesuit novitiate and seminary studies on March 24. As a young Jesuit scholastic, he suffered from repeated bouts of sickness. He would be sent home to recover, would return in robust health, then would come down with another ailment. Normally this would have been seen as a sign that he did not have a vocation, yet his superiors kept him on. Fr. Finn commented, "God often uses instruments most unfit to do His work

PREFACE

In presenting a second edition of Percy Wynn

to the boy and girl readers of America, the author, besides making a number of minor changes, has added two new chapters.

The author favors in a particular manner that portion of the thirteenth chapter where Martin Peters recalls to mind the catechism class of the preceding day; and thinks this the finest passage in his book. As he has borrowed the substance of this passage from the writings of Father Spec, S.J., a famous Jesuit, poet, and reformer of the sixteenth century, he feels no qualms of modesty in making this statement.

Should Percy Wynn and Tom Playfair find favor with young readers, their further adventures will be set forth very shortly in two supplementary volumes, "Tom Playfair," a tale in which are narrated the early adventures of Tom before meeting with Percy; and "Harry Dee, 5 ' a tale in which Tom and Percy are conducted through college and ushered into the great world.

FRANCIS JL FINN, S.J.

March I, 1891

PERCY WYNN

CHAPTER I

In Which Percy Wynn Bows to Thomas Play* fair and the Reader Simultaneously

Say, young fellow, what are you moping here for?" The person thus rudely addressed was a slight, delicate, fair-complexioned child, whose age, one could perceive at a glance, must have been something under fourteen. Previous to this interruption, he had been sitting solitary on a bench, in a retired corner of the college play-ground. That he was not a boy of ordinary characteristics was at once apparent. His eyes were large, fringed by long lashes; and their deep blue was intensified by his fair features. His face was an exquisite oval; it was one of those expressive faces which reveal in their every line the thoughts and emotions of the past. And his past must have been bright, and good, and pleasant; for amiability and confidence and innocence had written their traces on every feature. But the rosy cheek and the sunbeam's tint were conspicuously absent, and, in the matter-of-fact parlance of a school-fellow, his complexion and general appearance would be styled girlish. Nor would such appel

lation be entirely unjust. His hands were small, white, and delicate, while his golden hair fell in gleaming ripples about his shoulders. In perfect keeping with all this, his form was slight and shapely. Even his attire lent its art towards bringing into notice the slender grace of his figure. His neat coat, his knickerbockers which barely reached to the knee, his black silk stockings, and his high-laced shoes, while clearly revealing the nice proportion of his form, were agreeably set off and contrasted, in the soberness of their color, by a bright and carefully arranged neck-tie. No one, indeed, looking at him for a moment would hesitate to set him down as "Mamma's darling."

The boy who put him the question was one of a group, which had just broken upon the soli* tude of our little friend. He was a contrast i* every particular. Stout, freckle-faced, sandy-haired, impudent in expression, Charlie Rich* ards, it was at once evident, was something of a bully. There was an air of good-humor about his face, however, which was a redeeming trait. If he was a bully and consequently cruel, it was rather from thoughtlessness than from malice. If he was unkind, it was not that he lacked generous qualities, but rather because his feelings had been blunted by evil associates. He, too, was a new-comer at St. Maure's, having arrived on the opening class-day. Three weeks had already passed, and by his boldness and physical courage he had gathered about him a following of some nine or ten boys, all of whom were incipient bullies, several of them far more cruel, far more wicked in disposition than their leader.

PERCY WYNN

When this boy's question broke upon the child's ears, he raised his head, which had been buried in his hands, and gazed in undisguised fear upon the group before him. Evidently he had been so buried in his own thoughts and sorrows that their approach had failed to arouse him.

"Say, young fellow, don't you hear me?" continued Richards unsympathetically. "What are you moping here for?"

The boy's lips trembled, but he made no answer. He seemed, indeed, at a loss for words.

"Well, at least tell us what's your name," pursued Richards.

"Percy Wynn, sir."

His voice was clear and musical. The name evoked a low, derisive chuckling from the crowd.

"Percy Wynn ! Percy Wynn!" repeated Richards in a tone intended to be sarcastic. 'Why, it's a very, very pretty name. Don't you think so yourself?"

"Oh yes, indeedy !" answered Percy very seriously, whereupon there was a shout of laughter from the boys. As Percy perceived that his questioner had been mocking him, the blood rushed to his face, and he blushed scarlet.

"My! look how he blushes—just like a girl," cried Martin Peters, a thin, puny, weazen-faced youth, who in lieu of strength employed a bitter tongue.

There was another laugh; and as poor Percy realized that the eyes of nearly a dozen boys stfere feeding and gloating upon his embarrass-

ment, he blushed still more violently, and arising, sought to make his way through them, and escape their unwelcome company.

But Richards rudely clutched his arm.

"Hold on, Percy."

"Oh, please do let me go. I desire to be alone."

"No, no; sit down. I want to ask you some more questions." And Richards roughly forced him back upon the bench.

"Now, Percy, do you know where you're going to sleep to-night?"

"Yes, sir; over there in that—that—dormitory, I think the prefect said it was. He showed me my bed a little while ago."

"Very well; now you're a new-comer, and don't know the customs of this place. So I want to tell you something. To-night, just as soon as you get in bed— -and, by the way, you must hurry up about it— you must say in a loud, clear tone, Tut out the lights, Mr. Prefect; I'm in bed.' "

The listeners and admirers of Richards forced their faces into an expression of gravity. They were inwardly tickled: lying came under their low standard of wit.

"Oh, indeed!" said Percy. "Excuse me, sir, but can't you get some one else to say it?'

"No, no; you must say it yourself. It's the custom for new-comers to do it the first night they arrive."

"But, dear me!" exclaimed Percy, "isn't it a funny custom?"

"Well, it is funny," Richards -assented, "but it's got *-o be done all the same."

4 Very well, then; I suppose I must do it/'

"Now, do you remember what you are to say?"

"Tut out the lights, Mr. Prefect; I'm in bed/ "

'That's it exactly; you've learned your lesson well. Now there's another thing to be done. You must turn a handspring right off."

'Turn what ?" asked Percy in a puzzled tone.

"Look," and Richards suited the action to the word.

"Oh, upon my word," protested Percy in all earnestness, "I can't."

"No matter; you can try

"Oh, please dp excuse me, sir, this time, and I'll practice at it in private," pleaded Percy. "And when I've learned it, I'll be ever so glad to comply with your wishes."

'Whew!" exclaimed John Sornmers, "he's been reading up a dictionary!"

"Oh, indeed I haven't," protested Percy.

"Come on," Richards urged in a tone almost menacing, "you must try. Hurry up, now; no fooling."

Percy could endure his awkward position no longer. Bursting into tears, he rose and again attempted to make his way through his tormentors.

Richards caught him more rudely than upon the first occasion, and with some unnecessary and brutal violence flung him back upon the bench. "See here, young fellow," he said angrily, "do you want to fight? or are you going to do what you're told?"

"Of course he doesn't want to fight, and he'd

be a fool to do anything you tell him," said a new-comer on the scene, who brought himself through the thick of the crowd by dint of vigorous and unceremonious elbowing. "See here, Richards, it's mean of you to come here with your set and tease a new boy. Let him alone." And Master Thomas Playfair seated himself beside the weeping boy, and stared very steadily and indignantly into Richards' face. The bully's eyes lowered involuntarily, he hesitated for one moment, then, abashed, turned away.

Tom Playfair was an "old boy," this being his third year at St. Maure's. Now, to be an "old boy" is in itself, according to boarding-school traditions, an undoubted mark of superiority. Furthermore, he was the most popular lad in the small yard; and although Richards was older and somewhat more sturdily built than Tom, it would not do for him to come into collision with one so influential. So Richards sulkily withdrew, and was speedily followed by his companions, leaving Percy alone with Tom Playfair.

Tom Playfair! the same bright, cheerful, happy Tom whom some of my readers have already met. Just as healthy, stronger, a little taller; but the same kind, genial Tom. His sturdy little legs were still encased in knickerbockers, his rounded cheeks still glowed with health; his blue sailor-shirt still covered the same brave, strong heart.

For a few moments there was a silence, broken only by the sobs of Percy. Tom's right hand, meanwhile, was deep in his jacket-pocket.

Presently, when Percy had become calmer, it emerged filled.

"Here, Percy, take some candy."

Tom had a way of offering candy which was simply irresistible. No long speech could have had so reassuring an effect. Percy accepted the candy, and brightened up at once; put a caramel in his mouth, then drawing a dainty silk handkerchief from his breast-pocket, he wiped his eyes and broke into a smile which spoke volumes of gratitude.

'That's good," said Tom, encouragingly. "You're all right now. My name's Tom Play-fair, and I come from St. Louis. I know your name already, so you needn't tell me it. Are you a Chicago boy?"

"No, sir, I'm from Baltimore."

"See here," said Tom, "do you want me to run away?"

"No, indeedy!" said Percy, smiling, shaking back his long golden locks, and opening his eyes very wide. "Why, are you afraid of Baltimore boys?"

"It isn't that," Tom made answer. "But if you say 'sir' to me, I'll run away. Call me Tom and I'll call you Percy."

"Very well, Tom, I will. And I am very happy to make your acquaintance."

Tom was startled, and for a moment paused, not knowing what manner of reply to make to this neatly-worded compliment.

"Well," he said at length, "let's shake hands t then."

To his still greater astonishment, Percy gravely arose and with a graceful movement of his body, which was neither a bow nor a curtsy, but something between the two, politely took his hand.

"Well, I never!" gasped Tom. 'Where in the world did you come from?"

"From Baltimore, Maryland," said Percy. "I thought I had just told you."

"Are all the boys there like you?"

"Well, indeed, Tom, I really don't know. I wasn't acquainted with any boys, you know. Mamma said they were too rough. And"— here Percy broke almost into a sob —"they are rough, too. You're the only one of the boys I've met so far, Tom, that's been kind to me."

Tom whistled softly.

"Didn't know any boys?"

"Not one."

"Well, then, who on the round earth did you play with?"

"Oh, with my sisters, Tom. I have ten sisters. The oldest eighteen, and the youngest is six. Kate and Mary are twins. And oh, Tom, they are all so kind and nice. I wish you knew them; I'm sure you'd like them immensely."

Tom had his doubts. In his unromantic way, he looked upon girls as creatures who were to be made use of by being avoided.

"Did you play games with your sisters, Percy?"

"Oh yes, indeedy! And, Tom, I can dress a doll or sew just as nicely as any of them. And I could beat them all at the skipping-rope. Then we used to play 'Pussy wants a corner,' and 'Hunt the slipper,' and 'Grocery-store,' and I used to keep the grocery and they were the customers—and oh, we did have such times! And then at night mamma used to read to us, Tom—such splendid stories, and sometimes . beautiful poems, too. Did you ever hear the story of Aladdin and the Wonderful Lamp?"

"I believe not," said Tom modestly.

"Or Ali Baba and the Forty Thieves?"

Tom again entered a negative.

"Oh, they're just too good; they're charming. I'll tell them to you, Tom, some day, and a good many more. I know ever so many."

"I like a good story," said Tom, "and I'm sure I'll be very glad to listen to some of yours."

"Oh yes, indeedy! But, Tom, do you know why I've come here ? Our family has given up housekeeping. Poor, dear mamma has fallen into very delicate health, and has gone to Europe with papa for a rest. Papa has given up business, and intends, when he returns, to settle in Cincinnati. He has sent all my sisters to the school of the Sacred Heart there, except the oldest and the two youngest, who are staying with my aunt who lives on Broadway. But they've promised to write to me every day. They're going to take turns. Do your sisters write you regularly, Tom?"

"I haven't any sister," Tom answered, smiling. But there was just a touch of sadness in the smile.

"What! not a single one?"

Percy's expression was one of astonishment.

"Not one."

Astonishment softened into pity.

"Oh, poor boy!" he cried, clasping his hands in dismay. "How did you manage to get on?"

"Oh, I've pulled through. My mamma is dead too," said Tom, still more sadly.

The deep sympathy which came upon Percy's face at this declaration bespoke a tender and sympathetic heart. He said nothing, but clasped Tom's hand and pressed it warmly.

"Well, you are a good fellow!" broke out Tom, putting away his emotion under cover of boisterousness, "and I'm going to make a boy out of you/"

"A boy!" Percy repeated. 'Yes, a boy— a real boy."

"Excuse me, Tom; but may I ask what you consider me to be now?"

Tom hesitated. 'You won't mind?" he said doubtfully.

"Oh, not from you, Tom; you're ray friend."

"Well," said Tom, haltingly, "you're— Well, you're just a little bit queer, odd— girlish — that's it."

Percy's eyes opened wide with astonishment.

"You don't say! Oh, dear me! But Tom, it's so funny that I never heard I was that way before. My mamma and my sisters never told me anything about it."

"Maybe they didn't know any boys."

"Oh yes, they did, Tom. They knew me."

Percy considered this convincing.

'Yes, but you're not like other boys. They couldn't judge by you."

"Excuse me?" said Percy, still in great astonishment.

'You're not like other boys; not a bit."

"But I've read a great deal about boys. I've read the Boyhood of Great Painters and Musi-clans, and about other boys, too, but I can't remember them all now. Then I've read

Hood's

'Oh, when I was a little boy My days and nights were full of joy.'

Isn't that nice, Tom? I know the whole poem by heart."

It was now Tom's turn to be astonished. 'You don't mean to say," he said in a voice expressive almost of awe, "that you read poetry-books?"

"Oh yes, indeedy!" answered Percy with growing animation; "and I like Longfellow ever so much—he's a dear poet—don't you?"

Just then the bell rang for supper. Tom, absorbed in wonder, brought his new friend to che refectory, and, during the meal, could scarcely refrain from smiling, as he noticed with what dainty grace our little Percy took his first meal at St. Maure's.

CHAPTER II

In which Percy is Cross-examined by Thomas Play fair and Makes Some New Friends

U T_JARRY! Harry Quip!" shouted Tom as the boys came out from supper, "come here. I want to introduce you."

Harry, making his way out of the crowd, came forward, and was as sheepish as boys generally are on the occasion of an introduction.

"Harry Quip, this is a new boy all the way from Baltimore, and his name is Percy Wynn."

Harry put out his hand awkwardly enough. Suddenly the sheepishness upon his face crystallized into the most violent amazement, as graceful Percy, with his half-bow, half curtsy, distinctly enunciated:

"Mr. Harry Quip, I am charmed to make your acquaintance."

"He quotes poetry, too," said Tom in a low whisper to Harry, "and he uses bigger words than I've ever seen out of a book." He then added aloud: "Say, Harry, I wish you'd go and see to his desk and things in the study-hall; and when you're through, bring Joe Whyte and Will Ruthers along. I'll be down at the farther end of the yard with Percy. I want to have a little talk with him."

Harry was only too glad to get away, his face still expressing utmost astonishment, and his lips muttering in stupefied wonder: "And he quotes poetry, too!"

"Percy," began Tom as they sauntered down the yard towards a bench at the farther end, "did you ever play base-ball?"

"No; but I've heard about it."

"Did you ever play hand-ball?"

"Do you mean a returning ball, Tom? Oh, lots of times."

Tom did not mean a returning ball, but he went on.

"Did you ever handle a gun?"

"A real gun?"

"Of course. I don't mean a pop-gun or a broomstick."

"With real powder and real bullets!" exclaimed Percy in horror. "Oh, Tom! the idea!"

"Ever go fishing with a real hook and a real line?" Tom next inquired, mischievously employing Percy's turn of expression.

"No; but I'd like to, if someone would fix on the worm and take the fish off the hook."

"Did you ever go boating in a real boat, on real water?"

"Oh dear, no! Mamma said that boats tip so easily. She wouldn't have allowed me to get in one even if I wished."

"Did you ever go to a circus?"

"Once, Tom: Sister Mary, sister Jane, and myself with papa. And oh, wasn't it splendid! The clown was the funniest thing! He used to make such awfully queer remarks. I wondered where he got them all. After that I used to play circus at home. But really, I didn't succeed very well. I didn't dare try to imitate the clown, and most of the things I saw were too hard."

Tom was not yet through with his analysis. He thought of all the amusements of his ante-college days.

"Did you ever run to a fire ?"

"Oh no, indeedy!" said Percy.

"Can you swim?"

"I used to try in the bath-room at home, but the basin was too small. Mamma said it was dangerous to go in deep water."

Tom reflected for a moment. He was both amused and surprised.

"Well," he resumed after a silence, "most boys are pretty well up in all these things long before they get to be your age." 'You astonish me," said Percy.

"Let's look at your hands. Ah! I thought so. They're soft as—as mush. Here, now, I want you to do me a favor. Shut your hand tight—that's it—tighter still. Now hit me as hard as you can on the muscle — here!" And Tom, holding out his right arm, indicated the upper half.

"Oh, Tom, I don't want to hurt you!"

"Don't be alarmed; I'm tough," said Tom, smiling. "Go on, now, strike as hard as you can."

Percy brought his arm through the air in much the same manner as a woman when attempting to throw something; but as he neared Tom's arm, his courage failed.

'I can't do it. Oh, indeed I can't."

"Come on, all your might," said Tom.

Percy gave his arm another tremendous

swing; but he relented at the very last moment, and so his little knuckles came down on Tom's sturdy limb with a gentleness which was almost caressing.

"Don't pet me," said Tom in mock seriousness, "I'm not used to it. Pshaw! a fly wouldn't have known he was hit. Over again now, and just as hard as you can."

This time Percy, closing his lips firmly and chatting his eyes so as not to lose courage, brought his doubled fist with all the force he could muster against the extended arm.

There was a cry of pain.

But not from Tom.

"Oh laws!" Percy exclaimed, "I've hurt my hand."

Tom sat down upon the bench, and laughed till the tears came to his eyes.

"Why, you're the funniest boy I ever met."

"Am I ?" said Percy, doubtfully, and smiling in his perplexity. "Well, I'm glad you enjoy it. Oh, here comes Mr. Middleton," he continued. "He's a nice man, and I like him immensely. Good-evening, Mr. Middleton,"—he gracefully raised his hat and made his curious little bow, — "it's a beautiful evening, sir, isn't it?"

"Very nice indeed," the prefect made answer with a cheering smile. He was much amused by the quaint ways of the new student, although from delicacy he allowed his countenance to give no sign of his feelings.

"You didn't wait for me, Percy," he continued, "outside the dormitory after I gave you your bed; and so I had no opportunity of introducing you to some of the boys before supper.

But I've noticed already that you seem able tc make your own way."

"I don't like boys, Mr. Middleton."

"Indeed! that's strange. You're a boy yourself."

"Yes, sir, but I can't help that; I like girls better."

"Do you?"

"Yes, indeedy! My sisters are ever so much nicer than boys."

"But perhaps you don't know many boys." 'Well, that's so, sir. There were a few here came up to me just before supper, and they were awfully rough. Indeed, if it hadn't been for Tom, I don't know what I'd have done. But I do like Tom, Mr. Middleton; I like him just as if he was Pancratius."

Tom blushed at the compliment, and was puzzled by the comparison.

"So you've read Fabiola, Percy?" pursued the prefect.

"Oh yes, indeedy, every word of it! Isn't it a beautiful book? And St. Agnes! I did like her. And do you remember the little boy who was carrying the Blessed Sacrament concealed in his bosom and died rather than let the pagans desecrate and insult it? Oh, that was so noble! He was a hero!"

"Clearly this is an extraordinary lad," thought the prefect. "Under all his odd, quaint, girlish ways there is hidden a beautiful soul. He has fallen in, too, with the very boy who will best help to his development."

With a few words of encouragement and a friendly smile, Mr. Middleton left them. Pres-

ently Harry appeared, bringing with him Joe Whyte and Willie Ruthers. After the same startling bow consequent on the formality of introduction had awakened the wonder of the new-comers, a conversation began which, drifting here and there, was finally closed by Tom's proposing a story.

Without the least hesitation, Percy related the adventures of Ali Baba with the immortal forty thieves. Certainly his fluency and animation were wonderful. He spoke in tones beautifully modulated, and employed words which — to borrow Harry Quip's subsequent remark— "would give an ordinary boy the lockjaw." In the heat of narration, too, he made gestures which were markedly elegant. In short, the whole proceeding was so extraordinary that the listeners, while fairly carried away by the interest of the story, could not but glance at each other from time to time in silent wonder.

For full twenty-five minutes did the young narrator engage their attention! and when the bell sounded for studies the listeners all agreed that they had rarely spent so pleasant an evening. Girlish of manner, odd of speech, dainty of gesture, though our little Percy was, he had yet found his way into the hearts of Tom and his friends.

That night Mr. Middleton was quietly reading in the dormitory while the boys were slipping into bed, when a clear, sweet voice broke the stillness.

"Put out the lights, Mr. Prefect; I'm in bed."

Mr. Middleton arose from his chair, and swept the whole length of the dormitory with his eye. There was a general smile, but no loud laughter. Poor little Percy, dreadfully alarmed at the sound of his own voice breaking upon the silence, shut his eyes tight. Of course, he could scarcely hear the smiles, and so, as everything was quiet, he had no reason to think that his proceedings had been in any wise irregular. And thus very soon the singular child fell asleep, with those sacred names upon his lips which a fond mother, bending nightly over the bedside of her child, had taught him to utter in all confidence, innocence, and love.

CHAPTER III

In which Percy has a Strange Midnight

Adventure

A T half-past five next morning, the wash-room of the junior students literally swarmed with boys, while their number was constantly swelled by fresh additions from the dormitory. There was no talking in the room, but the clatter of basins, the splash and ripple and gurgle of water, the sibilant noise of many brushes, and, like a refrain, the hurried movement to and fro of little lads in all the various stages of incomplete toilet, gave the apartment an air of animation and crowded life which to an uninitiated onlooker was really refreshing.

As Percy descended the stairs of the dormitory, the sight certainly struck him with a sense of novelty. Boys pulling on coats, boys taking them off, boys baring their arms, boys blacking their shoes, boys brushing their clothes, boys combing their hair, boys lathering their heads till their figures looked like so many overgrown snowballs mounted on live, moving legs—boys, boys, boys, in every conceivable attitude, made up a scene charged with life, vigorous with bustling variety.

In matters of toilet Percy was perfectly at home. So without hesitation or inquiry he filled his basin and acquitted himself of his ablutions

with the neatness and precision of an expert. But when it came to arranging his tie he glanced around the wash-room till finally he espied Tom.

"Good-morning, Tom," he said, addressing that young gentleman, who was making energetic endeavors to get some injudiciously applied soap out of his eye. "Why, you are a perfect fright! You don't know how to comb your hair at all. Let me fix it."

There was a titter among the boys in the immediate vicinity, and Tom, having rid himself of the soap, laughingly handed over his comb and brush to Percy.

"Your hair doesn't look nice when you comb it flat, Tom. I'll make it a little puffy; I am sure it will improve your appearance wonderfully. Hold your head still, you naughty boy. There, now, it's done, and you look ever so much improved. But look here, Tom ! YouVe got on that same tie I noticed yesterday. The idea of wearing a blue tie on a blue shirt ! Why, they don't set each other off at all. Let me see.'

He stood off a few feet from Tom, and examined him critically.

"Oh yes. Yellow goes well with blue, and I've a beautiful golden tie, which I'm going to give you."

"Percy," said Mr. Middleton.

Percy turned, and found the prefect beside him, with his finger to his lips.

"Oh, excuse me, Mr. Middleton, I really beg your pardon. I just wished to fix Tom up a little. I forgot all about silence. I won't speak loud any more."

Tripping over to the wash-box, he quickly returned with the "beautiful golden tie," which, with a few dexterous folds, he tied into what is popularly called, I believe, a "butterfly." This bewitching decoration added a new and unusual grace to Tom's naturally pleasing appearance. 'There!" whispered Percy, with the enthusiasm of an artist, "you look ever so much improved. Now fix my tie."

"I'm afraid it's not in my line," Tom answered modestly.

"Don't you know how to fix a tie? I thought everybody knew that."

"I never had any sisters to teach me," suggested Tom.

"Oh, so you didn't. Well, it doesn't matter. I'll get Mr. Middleton to do it,—he's so nice."

Before Tom could remonstrate or otherwise express his astonishment, Percy calmly walked over to Mr. Middleton, who was standing at the end of the room, beside the dormitory steps.

"Mr. Middleton, will you kindly fix on my tie? I'm not used to doing it myself. Sister Mary always did it. I asked Tom to help me, but he doesn't know how."

The prefect smiled at his unusual request, and, accepting the tie, arranged it to the best of his ability, while Percy, in his polite way, took it entirely as a matter of course.

"Many thanks, Mr. Middleton: I don't think I'll have to trouble you again, for I intend to teach Tom how to do it to-day." And with his peculiar bow Percy left the wash-room.

Mass and studies before breakfast passed away without incident worthy of notice, Dur-
ing the Holy Sacrifice, Percy impressed those near him with his modesty and reverence. He had a richly bound, clasped prayer-book, which he evidently knew how to use.

After breakfast he called Tom, Harry, Willie, and Joe to accompany him to the trunk-room.

"I've got something for each one of you," he said, smiling gayly, as they entered the precincts of the clothes-keeper.

From his trunk he produced a perfumed box, and, opening it, revealed to their glances of admiration a number of pretty silk handkerchiefs. 'Take your choice," he said.

"Nonsense !" protested Tom, "we're not brigands. Keep them yourself, Percy."

But Percy so lost countenance at this refusal, and protested so earnestly that nothing would please him more than their each accepting one, that Tom, Harry, Willie, and Joe were fain at length to yield. Nor was Percy yet satisfied. He insisted on instructing each of them how and where to carry his gift; and when all, after due direction, stood before him with the least little tip of handkerchief just peeping over their breast-pockets, he clapped his hands.

But Tom put an end to these proceedings.

"Now it's my turn, Percy. Come to the yard, and I'll teach you a trick or two."

To the yard they went in a body.

"Now," Tom remarked a moment later, "spread your legs just the least little bit so as to make yourself steady, and bend your head till your chin touches your chest." Percy complied.

"Now be sure to stand steady, or you'll tumble."

'What are you going to do, Tom?" By way of answer, Tom, bracing himself lightly on Percy's shoulders, leaped clean over him, much to that young gentleman's astonishment, who, after having recovered his partially lost balance, anxiously asked Tom whether he was hurt.

"Bosh!" said Tom. "You can do it yourself."

"Oh dear, no!"

"But you can try."

"I'd be sure to fall on my head, and dirty my clothes; and besides," laughed Percy, venturing on a joke, "I might spill out all my ideas."

"Oh, go on," urged Harry Quip. "Joe and I will stand on the other side, and be ready to catch you if you fall."

Tom had already (to use the technical expression of the small boy) "made a back for him."

"Oh, I can't," said Percy. "It's too high.' 1 'Well, I'll stoop lower, then;" and Tom, bringing his arms below his knees and clasping his hands, doubled himself up. 'That looks easier," said Percy.

Compressing his lips and summoning all his resolution, Percy drew off some fifty feet, then at a great run he cleared Tom's back without, as he had anticipated, "spilling his ideas."

"Oh, that's glorious !" he cried. "Let me try ft again."

The experiment was repeated over and over until Percy, who had rarely indulged In exercise

more violent than fast walking, was completely out of breath. But he was proud of his success, and the sympathetic encouragement which his playfellows evinced so added to his happiness that, while his countenance was flushed from the exhilarating exercise, it beamed also with the double happiness of being pleased and of pleasing. Leapfrog came upon him like a revelation ; it opened new and undeveloped possibilities in his life.

'•'Is that the kind of games boys have?" he asked when he had recovered breath sufficiently to speak.

"Oh, that's nothing extra," said Joe Whyte. "It's nothing at all to some games."

"You ought to see Foot-and-a-half," said Willie.

"Or Bom-bay," added Harry Quip.

"And Base-ball," Tom chimed in, "is better than all of them put together."

'You don't say! Well, I declare! You astonish me," said Percy. "And now I'm glad I'm a boy."

"That's sensible," said Tom; "and the older you get the gladder you'll be."

Tom had decided views on this point.

Presently Percy was called away by the prefect of studies to be examined. On his return, Tom and Harry were delighted at learning that he was to be their classmate. They were both in the second Academic, a class in which Greek is begun, and Latin continued from the preceding year.

During class, that morning, Percy listened with great attention. The "Viri Romae" which he vainly tried to make out, as the boys translated and parsed it line by line, troubled him not a little.

Towards the end of the class, he said aloud:

"Mr. Middieton, don't you think that the study of Latin is attended with considerable difficulties for a beginner?"

The boys were too astounded to laugh.

"It is hard at first," admitted the professor with a smile. 'There's a proverb, you kno\v, which says, 'knowledge makes a bloody entrance.' Still the more you learn of it the more you will like it, and the easier, too, will it be-

come."

U'

'Thank you, sir," said Percy. "I believe what you say, though it has never struck me that way before. I know it's true in English studies —the more I read the more I love to read. Oh, Mr. Middieton, won't you please tell us a story?"

Percy spoke as he would have spoken to his mother or sisters. Not a little to bJs astonishment, then, this sudden and unlooked-for request was greeted with a general burst of taugh-ter.

Mr. Middieton smiled, and "put the question by," in requesting one of the students to parse the fourth line of the lesson.

Charlie Richards was a member of the class, and his attention and contempt were strongly roused by the singular remarks of the newcomer.

"What a silly innocent that fellow is!" he reflected. "He must have been tied to his? mother's apron-string. I think we can get some fun out of him."

Richards' course of thinking was not in vain. At recess he held a whispered consultation with Peters.

"We'll scare the wits out of him," said Richards when he had fully developed his plot.

"Oh, it'll be great fun!" chuckled Peters, rubbing his skinny hands together. "I'll fix up your face so you'll look like an awful ghost. I'll put red paint about your eyes, and blacken the rest of your face, so that you'll just frighten him into fits."

For a long time did these two weigh and consider the plans for their vile practical joke. Their innocent victim, meanwhile, was adding to his stock of experiences things to him altogether new.

In the recreation hour after dinner, Tom produced a base-ball.

"See that, Percy."

"Oh, what a hard ball!" cried Percy, touching it in a gingerly way.

'Well, you've got to learn to catch it."

"I? no, indeedy! it's just like a rock. My poor little fingers would be ruined, and then, Tom, I wouldn't be able to play the piano."

"Halloa! can you play the piano?"

"Yes, indeedy! I just love it. And I can sing, too."

'Why, you know everything I don't know, and don't know anything I do."

Percy laughed.

"My sisters taught me," he said, as he shook back his sunny locks.

"Did they teach you to say, 'Yes indeedy! 1

Cn inHppHv!'?" nneripH Tntm clvlv

*No, indeedy!'?" queried Tom, slyly.

"Oh la! how you do notice things ! 'Indeedy 1 isn't good grammar, I know."

"It's worse yet," said Tom; "it's girlish."

"You don't tell me!" cried Percy, his blue eyes opening to their widest. "Now I know why everybody laughs when I say it. Thank you, Tom, ever so much. I'll stop using it."

"But what about this ball? You must learn to catch it."

"Catch that ball! I'd as lief catch a cannon-ball. Oh no, indeedy!—that is," he said, catching himself— "that is, indeed I won't."

"Oh, it's not so hard," said Tom. "Here, I'll make it easy for you, and show you how it's done, too. Take the ball and walk off about twenty paces from me, then throw^ it as hard as you can at me, and see me catch it."

"But you mustn't be put out if I hurt you," pleaded Percy, as he took his stand at the assigned distance.

"I'll take all risks," said Tom in great glee.

Percy with the ball in his right hand, made q. feint of throwing it.

"Don't balk," said Tom. "Throw it as hard as ever you can. If it's too swift"— here Tom was obliged to pause that he might suppress a laugh —"I'll dodge it.'

There was no necessity for "dodging," however.

Percy whirled his arm round and round, and at length let the ball fly from his hand. He trembled for the consequences; not, indeed, without reason. The ball, instead of going towards Tom, went some thirty or forty feet wide of him (were he a giant he could not have "covered so much ground"), and seemed to be making straight for the head of John Donnel, who, with his hands in his pockets, was evincing the deepest interest in the progress of a game of hand-ball.

"Look out, John!" roared Tom. "Duck your head." The warning came just^ in time. By a quick movement John succeeded in receiving the ball on the back of his head instead of in the face.

"Well, I never!" he said rubbing the injured part. As he spoke, a piercing, startling scream broke upon his ears. It was from Percy.

"Oh, poor boy!" he cried, running over to John, tears of sympathy standing in his eyes.

"I must have hurt you very much,, But, upon my honor, I didn't mean it, sir. Indeed I didn't: did I,Tom? Oh, sir, please tell me you're not seriously hurt. Really and truly, I'm awfully mortified."

If the ball had surprised John, this sympathetic and eager address, coming from the lips of a dainty little lad whom he had never met before, astounded him.

"Oh, I'm dreadfully hurt," he said with rnock solemnity. "I suppose somebody will have to carry me over to the infirmary."

"Oh la! deary me!" wailed Percy. Toor boy! Tom and I will carry you anywhere you wish. Tom, you catch his feet, and I'll take his head. Oh, sir, only say you'll forgive me."

And Percy was on the point of crying.

"Why, you little goose, you don't mean to

say you honestly think I'm hurt?" laughed the great second-baseman of the small yard, as he perceived that Percy was taking him seriously. "I'm not hurt a bit. Of course I forgive you; and whenever you feel particularly inclined to amuse yourself, you can come and throw your ball at me again."

'Then there'd be no danger of your being hit," said Tom, gravely. "He won't hit the fellow he's aiming at; it's the other fellow."

Percy, relieved of his fears, joined in the laugh.

"Won't you introduce me?" suggested Percy.

"Certainly. John Donnel, this is Percy Wynn." The bow and the polite little speech were gone through in Percy's best form.

John was amused and charmed. Not only was he the largest boy in the yard, he was also the most genial. So well established was the kindliness of his disposition that he was styled "the little boys' friend." He readily divined Tom's ideas with regard to "making a boy, a real boy," of Percy; and in pursuance of this, he set to work actively at showing Percy how to use his arm in throwing.

A half-hour's practice, and, under the dexterous tuition of Tom and John, Percy succeeded in so directing the ball's path as to make it comparatively safe for the prudent bystander.

"That's enough for to-day," said Tom at length. "To-morrow your arm will be stiff a little, but you needn't mind that. It's always the way till you get used to it."

The reader (who is doubtless "a boy—a real boy") must have felt, in reading these pages, that Percy has said and done some very foolish things. Our little hero's judgment with regard to jumping, ball-tossing, and school-boy life in general must have appeared ridiculous even to the intelligence of a lad of seven. But imagine a man, say a fine musician, who, born blind and living in darkness for long, long years, has, on a sudden, his sight restored him. As a musician, he would appear as rational as ever; but as a gazer on the wonders of earth and starry sky he would be as an infant; more carried away than a little toddler of five attending the Christmas pantomime for the first time. One unacquainted with his previous condition would take him for a madman. Percy's case is somewhat similar. He was bright, clever, accomplished in matters where most young students are in utter darkness. But in practical knowledge of boys and boy-life he was little more than an infant. Everything about him was a subject of fear or of wonder, of dismay or of delight.

And so the day passed pleasantly enough. Night came, and Percy, thoroughly wearied from his unwonted exercise, fell into a profound slumber almost as soon as his head touched the pillow.

He had been sleeping for nearly two hours, when he was partially awakened by some one touching his feet. Turning restlessly on his side, he was again about to drift into dreamland, when a low, blood-curdling groan brought him to his full senses. Raising his head on his arm, he looked about him. Just at the foot of the bed, a terrible figure met his view—a sheeted form, draped in white. The eyes of the figure were hideous; some sort of a dim light playing about its face revealed the horrid black features.

Have any of you, my dear readers, ever seen a face under the influence of utter terror? The starting eyeballs, the open mouth, the ashen-pale countenance? Have you ever heard the wild shriek of horror from the lips of one thoroughly terrified?

Richards, the ghost, expected all these things, and, as Percy sat upright in his bed, gave another blood-curdling groan.

A clear, silvery laugh was heard.

Could his ears deceive him? Was the timid, girlish victim actually laughing? He groaned again.

"Ha, ha, ha! Oh my! it's as good as the circus. Oh la ! what a guy!"

Percy Wynn, seated in his bed, was laughing most merrily, and clapping his hands in unaffected glee.

But the disturbance awoke several near by, among them Harry Quip, whose bed was besicU Percy's. Now, Harry was by no means so im pressed with the fun of the thing as his merr\'7d little neighbor. He perceived at once that some brutal fellow had been trying to frighten Percy. Without ceremony, he jumped from his bed, seized the ghost, who by the way, contrary to the traditions of all ghosts, was the most thoroughly frightened of the company, and with a vigorous grasp brought his ghost-ship to the floor.

Although Charlie Richards had arranged himself with exceeding care for his assumed character, and even made such preparations as would enable him to slip back into his bed ere Percy's scream of horror should have died away, he had certainly not taken into consideration the possibility of being knocked down. In such event, a lighted candle, placed in the headdress so as to throw a dismal glare upon the ghostly features, is a decided inconvenience.

As the boy came violently to the floor, he gave a howl of pain and terror.

"Help! help!" he shouted. "I'm on fire."

His statement appeared to be true: the sheet was burning. At once the dormitory, one moment before all buried in silence, awoke to a scene of wild confusion. Every one was awake; every one was in motion.

"Get some water!" "Wake Mr. Middle-ton!" "Get a priest!" "Fire! fire!" Such and a thousand other like exclamations came from all sides. One timid little lad ran to the nearest window and began calling wildly for the police, forgetting in his bewilderment that St. Maure's village was a quarter of a mile distant, and that the only policeman it could boast was now, good old man, snug in bed.

Many fell upon their knees; others, still more panic-stricken, made a mad rush for the stair. Beside the door opening on the staircase wa? Mr. Middleton's bed. He was a sound sleeper, but, very luckily for the limbs if not the lives of those who were attempting to escape, he woke and sprang from his bed just in time to confront the foremost in the wild rush. Mr. Mid-dleton took in the situation at once. He was a humane man, and rarely acted in. haste. But

on this occasion there was time neither for thought nor explanation. With a violent shove he sent the nearest fugitive sprawling on the floor.

"Back!" he shouted commandingly, "back, every one of you !"

The panic was reversed. All turned and fled from the door, and Mr. Middleton, who had perceived the poor ghost's predicament, snatched up a blanket and hastened down the central aisle.

But Tom Playfair had anticipated him. Rushing forward with all his bedclothes, he threw himself on the -luckless ghost; and with such energy did he give himself to the work, that he not only extinguished the incipient flames, but also was within a little of suffocating the object of his zeal.

Richards' hair was badly singed, and part of his face scorched. Still wrapped in Tom's bedclothes, he was literally bundled over to the infirmary.

Order was soon restored: sleep, so kindly to youth, quickly reasserted her power, and the remaining hours of the night passed as quietly as though al) th-? ghosts of the earth had been laid forever.

CHAPTER IV
In which Peters and Percy Hold a Fery Odd
Conversation
I T WAS the morning following the ghost's dis-comfiture. The students had nearly all

deserted the washroom, when a sorry little figure, the picture of misery, came limping down the st3 1 rc3.se

u Oh, Mr. Middleton, I'm awfully sick. I don't know what's the matter with me. Do I look bad, sir?"

"Well, Percy, your face looks the same as usual; but you walk somewhat more stiffly. Where do you feel ill?"

u Oh, most everywhere."

"Did the ghost make you sick?"

u Oh, is that what the poor boy intended to play? I thought he just wanted to make me laugh: he did look so ridiculous! Oh no, in-deedy! —I beg your pardon—Oh no, indeed! he didn't scare me one bit."

"But where do you feel pain?"

"My legs are so stiff I can hardly walk. Then my right arm aches dreadfully, and my shoulder-blade is sore, too."

"I know your trouble, Percy," said Mr. Middleton, breaking into a smile of relief. 'You played more than usual yesterday, didn't you?"

"Oh yes, indeedy! — I mean yes, sir. I never took so much exercise before in all my life."

"That's It precisely. Your muscles have not been accustomed to such strains. You'll be all right if you keep quiet for a day or two. This morning you are really too stiff to go about at all, so I'm going to allow you a late sleep. You may go back to the dormitory now, and after breakfast I'll send Tom Playfair to awake you."

"Oh, thank you, sir. I'm so tired, I just feel as if I could sleep for a week. Mr. Mid-dleton, do you think I am much like a girl?"

'Well, in some respects you are." The prefect was nigh overcome at this abrupt and singular question.

"Ah! I thought so," said Percy, who seemed
in nowise discouraged at this candid answer.
'Tom Playfair said the same thing, and he's
so honest. Mr. Middleton, do you think it's
wrong to act like a girl?"

'The question never occurred to me in exactly that light before," answered Mr. Middle-ton, highly amused. "Of course, if a person can't help acting like a girl, I can't blame him." 'Well, it's not convenient. I think everybody looks at me as if I were a curiosity. Couldn't you suggest some changes in me, Mr. Middle-ton, to avoid being stared at? I hate to be stared at; don't you?'

"I am not fond of it, certainly."

The prefect could not but reflect that Percy's long golden hair helped much towards giving him a girlish appearance. Indeed, he was on the point of advising his questioner to rid himself of this feminine adornment, but he refrained from giving the idea words.

"The poor lad," he reflected, "might find it
a bitter trial just now. Probably his mamma and sisters thought much and made much of that head of golden hair, and Percy, with such memories fresh upon him, might consider its loss desecration. But even if I say nothing at present, the idea will still probably occur to him at some better time."

The prefect's decision was no less kind than judicious. He added aloud:

"Well, Percy, the best advice I can give you is to harden your muscles and strengthen your frame with plenty of out-door exercise. Take Tom Playfair for your guide in these matters, and very, very soon people won't care in the least about staring at you. Now go to bed. Some other time we'll have a longer talk on the same subject."

'Thank you very much indeed, Mr. Middle-ton. Good-by, sir;" and with a most unsuccessful attempt at his neat little bow, Percy made his way up to the dormitory.

Mass and studies over, Tom awoke him. After his second sleep, Percy found himself much better, but so stiff withal as to preclude all ideas of his taking further exercise, at least for that day.

"As you like reading," said Tom when Percy had finished his breakfast, "I'd advise you to read. Sit down on some bench, and take it easy. I'll come round now and then to see that you're all right."

'You mustn't trouble yourself about me at all, Tom. I'm just as happy as can be when I've a book to my liking. And I've got some* thing splendid now— 'Dion and the Sibyls.'

Mamma says It is, perhaps, the best Catholic novel ever written in the English language."

"Well, read away," said Tom. "I wish I liked reading as well as you. Most books make me weary. I haven't read hardly anything ex« cept 'The Miser,' and 'The Poor Gentleman,' and a few short stories." And Tom, almost sighing at his want of taste in literary matters, tripped away to fulfil an engagement at the hand-ball alley, leaving Percy seated contentedly on a bench in the delightful company of his cherished volume.

But he was not long undisturbed. Martin Peters, the accomplice of Richards in the unsuccessful apparition of the night, had puzzled much over Percy's character. He had never met, never imagined such a boy. He had seen Percy blush and tremble in the face of an impudent question, he had noted his alarm at the prospect of vaulting over Tom Playfair, and he had contemplated with no little glee his fear and anxiety on hitting John Donnel with the ball. All these traits had led him to believe that Percy was a coward. Hence he had confidently and jubilantly counted on Percy's going almost into hysterics at the sight of Richards in his spectre-attire. But Percy's laughter and glee upon confronting the spirit had dashed all his theories. Could it be that the girlish lad was not a coward? Impossible! What, then, might be the explanation of his seeming bravery? Perhaps, Peters reflected, he had been forewarned; perhaps, even he had overheard himself and Richards discussing their plans. Peters was a wily lad—a young Ulysses—and

he determined to explore to its depths the mystery of Percy's courage.

"Good-morning, Wynn," he began, seating himself beside the odd Baltimore boy, and trying to smile pleasantly, "you're having a read, I

see."

Percy closed his volume.

"Yes; I've a nice book. It's 'Dion and the Sibyls.' Have you read it?"

"No," said Peters.

"Oh, you ought to. It's delicious. Some of the scenes are described so nicely that you Would think you were on the spot, witnessing everything yourself. Aren't you fond of fine descriptions?"

"I like them well enough," said Peters, who, as a matter of fact, had never given the sub-i'ect a moment's thought. "But see here, Wynn, came to talk about something else. I heard you saw a ghost last night."

Percy broke into a musical laugh.

"Oh dear, no! It was one of the boys who wanted to have a little fun. He did make me laugh, and I'm really sorry he got hurt. I'm sure he meant no harm."

"Don't you think he wanted to frighten you?" queried Peters, much astounded at this simple view of the case.

"Surely not," said Percy. "It is extremely cruel and unkind to attempt to scare a person badly, and I don't believe Richards would think of such a thing. He has a kind face. Tom Playfair says boys are just as good as girls. Now girls wouldn't act that way. My sisters never did anything mean, though they

used to play jokes on me, too. One time, sister Mary, who is the greatest joker of them all, told me to go to my room and put on my new shoes. When I tried to get them on, I found a pair of gloves, one in each. It was a splendid joke and we all enjoyed it very much."

Peters was not accustomed to this kind of conversation, nor were his faculties of wit and humor capable of appreciating a joke so innocent. He was disgusted. The boy, he thought, must be a simpleton.

'Well, but weren't you scared last night?"

"No, indeedy!—I mean not at all. Why should I be?"

"Aren't you afraid of ghosts?"

"Oh dear, no! ?! laughed Percy, throwing back his hair and shaking his head. "Ghosts don't bother people. Why, when I lie awake in my bed at night I never think of ghosts. But I do think of angels."

"You do?" said Peters, dubiously.

"Yes, indeedy!" answered Percy, warming wo his subject. "And I think there's more sense /n it. We know from our religion that we've each a guardian angel. But we don't know for certain that there are any ghosts around us. Besides, I'd rather see an angel than a ghost. There's only one thing would prevent me from wishing to see my angel."

"What's that?" asked the muddled Ulysses, realizing more and more that he was beyond his depth.

"Sin!" exclaimed Percy with great emphasis, "mortal sin! If I were to do anything very bad, I would fear meeting my angel's face of

reproach. But oh, how glad I'd be to see him if I were good! The angels must be very beautiful; don't you think so, sir?"

"Oh, I suppose so," answered Peters, irresolutely.

"Yes, indeedy!—I mean surely. One of the nicest books I ever read was Father Faber's 'Tales of the Angels.' Did you ever read it?"

"No," said Peters, more and more confounded.

"Oh, you must. IVe got it with me in my trunk, and I'll lend it to you. The stories are so sweet. Would you like to read it? It's much better than reading about ghosts. Mamma told me never to think of ugly or disagreeable things after my night prayers, but always of God or the angels. Don't you think that's a splendid idea?"

"Yes, I guess so," Peters made answer as he shambled off.

Poor Peters ! the pretty tnoughts which Percy had just communicated to him were very absurd from his point of view. The idea of talking about angels! He departed convinced that Percy was little more than a simpleton. Yet, do not suppose, my dear reader, that Percy's words were utterly thrown away. Peters departed knowing more of angels, knowing more of beauty, than he had ever known before. These pretty words of Percy's may again awake in Peters' heart, these pretty words may do much towards raising his soul from foulness and sin to the All-beautiful God.

Good words from pure, innocent hearts are never lost; they are seeds of rare flowers whose blossoms we shall behold beyond the grave

In which Percy Goes A-Fishmg

IT WAS Thursday morning, a full recreation-day. Percy had quite recovered from his sdffness, and, according to agreement, was about to start for the "lakes" on a day's fishing excursion.

Promptly after breakfast, John Donnel, George Keenan, who was John's inseparable friend and classmate, Harry, Tom, Percy, Willie, and Joe briskly issued from the college grounds, and set forward westward along the railroad-track.

"Oh, what a glorious morning!'* cried Keenan, taking in a full breath; "it makes one feel poetical."

Now George was a member of the Poetry class.

'Yes, indeedy!—I mean Oh yes," chimed in Percy.

'Full many a glorious morning have I seen Flatter the mountain-top with sovereign eye.' "

"See here, you young prodigy," said Donnol, "where's your mountain-top?"

"Oh, nowhere in particular. This Kansas country is all little hills. But the lines came to my head when George said 'glorious morning, 1

49

and I couldn't help saying them. Anyhow, just look at the village-roofs dancing in the light of the sun."

u As Tennyson says in his famous lyric of St. Maure's at Sunrise," George gravely remarked,

'The splendor falls on college walls, And village roof-tops new in story; The long light shakes across our lakes And the gay college lad leaps in glory. Blow, Kansas, blow, set the high cloudlets

flying:

Blow, cyclones; answer, breezes, sighing, sigh-ing, sighing.' "

"Are you sure, George, that Tennyson wrote that?" asked Percy, gravely.

"Well, to tell the truth," said George, laughing, "it's a joint composition. Tennyson and I did it together. He furnished the general outline, and I introduced a few details."

4 Oh, I see now," said Percy, brightening. "It's a parody.'^

"Just so," said Keenan.

"But isn't it a beautiful morning?" continued Percy. "So calm and bright. I like the sunshine and the pure air. Don't you, Tom?"

"Well, I reckon I do," answered Tom, who was still puzzling over Percy's Shakespearian quotation. Tom was by no means an introspective youth. He took the air and the sunshine for granted. He did enjoy them, but was not in the habit of asking himself why.

"By the way," Percy resumed, "how far are these lakes from the college?"

"Four miles by the railroad," Harry made

answer.

u

Oh la!" almost screamed Percy, "I must go back "

"Why?" "Why?" "What's the matter?" cried everybody.

"It would kill me to walk four miles. I never walked more than a mile in my life. Oh dear! I'm so sorry, because I counted on having such a nice time."

Percy deliberately sat down.

"Nonsense!" said sturdy Tom. "You don't know what you can do till you try."

"Oh, it's quite out of the question," said Percy, shaking his golden locks with decision. "I really couldn't think of such a thing."

"See here, you wretched little sloth, you crab-fish, you turtle," said John Donnel in good humored indignation, "do you know what I'll think of you if you don't get up and come on?"

"Nothing bad, I hope," said Percy, anxiously.

"I'll think you're a goose."

"Will you?" said poor Percy in dismay.

"I certainly will."

"I wouldn't like you to think me a goose, John.'

"I'll think you one, too," said Keenan.

"And I." "And I." "And I," volleyed the others.

"But I'd rather be a goose with two sound legs than a cripple," said Percy, argumenta-tively.

"Oh, come on," said Tom. "If you get tired out, John and George will brace you up.
PERCY WYNN
They're strong enough to carry you two miles without stopping."

"Well, I—I'll go. But you mustn't get vexed with me if I give out."

All protested that the event of his losing power of locomotion would give no offence—none in the least; and so Percy, taking heart, arose and moved forward.

Presently Tom remarked:

"Percy, you're going to break your record
now."

;'How's that, Tom?"

"See that milestone? You've already walked a mile, and are now beginning your second."

'You don't say!" cried Percy in great delight. "And really, I'm not tired one bit."

When they had gained the next milestone, in deference to Percy a halt was declared. But that young enthusiast protested that he felt able to walk forever, and it was only after some discussion, clinched by physical violence from Master Tom, that he could be induced to sit down.

'You were right, John," said Percy. "I was * goose. I am beginning to think that I'm dreadfully silly."

"Oh, you're learning fast enough," said John, encouragingly.

'Tell us another story, Percy," suggested Harry.

'I would if we intended to stay more than a few minutes."

'Well, then, sing us a song," Tom put m 0

; 'Hear, hear!" cried the two poets.

Percy smiled, threw back his hair, hummed
for a moment to himself, then in a clear, sweet voice sang —

"Oh, I'll sing to-night of a beautiful land In the lap of the ocean set," etc.

As he began, all listened in wonder and admiration. It was not so much that his voice was rich, sweet, and clear; not so much that the wording of the poem was beautiful in itself, and the melody extremely pathetic. What gave it a nameless charm was the wondrous feeling with which he sang. The sadness of the exile breathed.in every strain; the tears of the patriot gazing upon his country's ruins trembled in every note. Music and feeling and love and innocence had joined hands. To all present, the song was a revelation. Among the young singers of St. Maure's many had rich, many had sweet voices, but none of them enjoyed that rare gift of wedding feeling to music. They sang like the little birds—blithely, gayly. But here was a child who could quicken a strain with a beautiful, sensitive soul.

When he had finished, Keenan, whose eyes were suspiciously dimmed, grasped his hand.

"I'm of German descent myself," he said, "and I believe there's a little English in me, too. But there's not a greater Irishman on the globe to-day than I am."

"Percy," said Tom, "I'd give up all I know about base-ball to be able to do that."

"Sister Jane taught me," said Percy, modestly "I'm very glad you all liked it so much. I know lots of songs, and whenever you like it I'll be delighted to sing."

Percy was, in truth, gratified; his greatest pleasure—a noble trait—was to give pleasure to others.

When the boys resumed their way, nearly all of them were thinking of a beautiful land with beautiful rivers, but devastated by the cruel hand of pitiless, grasping tyranny. Action and reaction were taking their course. Percy developed them from within, they developed him from without. Percy was enlarging his muscles; they, their feelings. Under cover of his dainty, effeminate ways, he had since his arrival been unconsciously communicating new and noble thoughts to his kind playfellows, while they consciously and visibly had given him practical knowledge of true boyhood. To know him, Tom might have said, using the well-known saying, was a liberal education.

In the course of an hour the lake was gained. A snug spot where the trees threw their shade far into the water was selected and occupied as the party's fishing-ground; forthwith Tom presented Percy with a fishing-line all complete, and produced a worm from the common bait-can.

Percy took the wriggling creature charily enough, held it for a moment, and then with a shriek let it fall from his hand.

"Oh dear! oh dear! what'll I do?" 'You might pick it up," said the unsympathetic Tom. "It won't hurt you; it doesn't bite."

Percy, after many unsuccessful efforts, at length recovered his wriggling worm, and, re» prcssfng a desire to shiver, endeavored to impale it upon his hook. But the more he tried, the more the "conqueror worm" wriggled.

"Lie quiet, you nasty thing!" he ejaculated.

But Tom here came to his relief.

"It's easy enough to stop his squirming. I'll show you another trick, Percy."

Taking the obstinate worm in one hand, he gave it a vigorous slap with the other. The worm no longer wriggled, and Percy, naturally skilful of finger, easily baited his hook.

"Now," said Tom, "there's two kinds of fish here—small fish, such as perch and sunfish, and large fish, which are all mostly mudcat. The mudcats are harder to manage; they've got mouths like stable-doors, and get the hook way down near their tail and seem to think it good eating."

"Yes," Quip chimed in, "and they're awfully insulted when you try to get it out."

"And if they get a chance, they'll stick you with their fins," said Whyte.

"Oh, gracious! I don't want to catch catfish," said Percy.

"You needn't try," said Tom; "and likely you won't. They keep out in the deep water; so to begin with, I'd advise you to throw in near shore, and you'll catch a perch. Try by that log over there, just sticking out of the

water.'

Percy followed these directions accurately. Hardly had his cork come to a firm stand on the face of the water when it began to jerk about In a most unsteady way.

Tom was entirely intent on arranging his own line.

"Oh, look at my cork, Tom! What's the matter with it?"

"It's drunk," said that worthy without looking up.

"Don't be ridiculous, Tom, but please look."

"You've got a nibble, Percy."

"A what?"

"A nibble. There's a fish holding an inquest on your worm." And Tom with a vigorous cast sent his line thirty feet or more into the water.

"Say, Tom!"

"Well, go on and say it."

"I—I think my cork is lost. I can't see it at all."

"Pull in!" Tom exclaimed with all the excitement of an enthusiast. "Always pull in when your cork goes under; there's a fish on it, sure."

Perhaps Percy had a vague impression that it was a whale or some huge monster of the deep; perhaps he was merely in a high state of excitement. At any rate he communicated a violent jerk to his line. Up flew his hook, with a tiny and such-surprised fish on it; up, up into the branches of the tree under which they were stationed.

The poor little fish floundered helplessly, and with each struggle entangled himself the worse. It was a question which was more perplexed, Percy or the tiny perch.

"Come down, little fishy," said Percy, coax-ingly, "Oh, do !"

Probably "little fishy" was as anxious to "come down" as was his captor.

"Put some salt on 'little fishy's' tail," said Quip in a tone of concern.

"Are you in earnest?" asked Percy, doubtfully.

"He's talking nonsense," said Donnel, straining every muscle to keep a straight face. "I'll tell you what you might do, Percy. Go to the nearest farm-house and borrow an axe. You can cut the tree down, and then you've got your fish."

"Oh dear!" said Percy, "I never used an axe in all my life."

"You ought to learn, then," Keenan put in. "Gladstone spends a great deal of his time felling trees."

"Oh, what shall I do?" cried the young fisherman. "Do you think he will come down, John?"

"I'm sure he'd like to, if he only knew how. But he doesn't. Are you good at handling tangles?"

"I think so," was Percy's modest answer. "I used to help sister Kate with her cotton-balls and skeins."

"Well, up you go, then," said the stout John. He caught Percy from the ground in his arms, then securing a sure hold on his high shoes, raised him into the air.

Two days before, Percy would have screamed with dismay. Now, however, the leap-frog experience stood him in good stead, and so, with scarcely a tremor, he caught the branch and very deftly extricated the entangled line and the struggling fish.

"Oh, John," he said as the good-natured poet lowered him to the ground, u you're a perfect Hercules. Thank you ever so much. But how do you get this fish off ?"

"See!" said John. "You catch him firmly round the head this way—now he can't slip. Then you push the hook smartly back, and pull it out so." John accompanied these lucid directions with practical example.

"Sh!" whispered Tom, suddenly, "I've a splendid bite. Just look at my cork, will you?"

His float was indeed acting strangely. Instead of bobbing up and down, or giving a series of queer little jerks, or sinking altogether, as a float generally does when under the influence of a fish-bite, it was moving steadily along the face of the water out from the land. Tom's pole was adorned with a reel: to afford the innocent victim more play, he gave out ten or twelve feet of line, and in great excitement dashed his hat to the ground. Still moved the cork steadily on—no jerking, no passing disappearance; it was as slow and regular in it^ phlegmatic onward movement as a policeman.

All the boys, forgetting their proper lines, were gazing with breathless attention.

"It's the funniest bite I ever saw," said Ker

nan.

It's not a catfish, sure," added Donnell, posk tively.

'What'll I do?" whispered Tom, giving out more line. "Why on earth doesn't the fish take

it or leave it? It's the worst fool of a fish I know of. I'll bet that fish hasn't sense enough to come in out of the rain. Will that cork ever stop moving out?' 1

"Look, look!" cried Ruthers in an excited whisper. "The cork is beginning to move in a circle."

As a matter of fact, the bobbin had changed its direction. For a moment its course had an air of hesitancy, then, of a sudden, it proceeded to come straight in towards the land.

'That fish is a lunatic!" said Quip, severely.

"Maybe it's no fish at all," suggested Whyte, taking a larger view of the matter.

"Perhaps it's a horrid snake," volunteered Percy, who looked as though he were prepared to take to his heels.

"Steady, Tom; bring in all the line you don't need," advised Keenan. "If you give too much of a slack, your game may smash the whole thing with a running jerk."

"Boys," said Tom, after reeling in his line some twenty feet, "I'm going to pull in. If that fish hasn't got sense enough to act like any ordinary decent fish and take a good square bite, I can't afford to lose my time fooling with it."

Tom gave his rod a strong and rapid upward jerk. Neither fish nor line came flying from the water. His rod simply bent almost double, and indeed threatened , to break.

"I knew it," said Tom, sighing and releasing the strain on it. "I'm caught fast on a log."

"No, you're not !" bawled Keenan, forgetting the orthodox fisherman's whisper in his extreme

excitement. "For goodness' sake, just look at your cork now!"

There never was a bobbin known to act so curiously. It was again moving straight out, but so swiftly that to Tom's excited imagination it seemed to be making a good forty miles an hour. Even in the moment of watching, his reel gave an impatient movement as if it desired to be free. Tom let it go, and off flew the line headed by the cork, which seemed to be gaining in liveliness every instant. 'The cork is crazy," said Whyte.

"It's bewitched, maybe," cried Ruthers.

"Catch the cork, Tom, and put some salt on its tail." This exquisite advice came from none other than Percy. The little lad was so frightened, and at the same time so excited, that, in the exhilaration produced by the blending of these feelings, he made the absurdest and most unlooked-for remark we have yet recorded as coming from him.

Suddenly the float came to a rest. Everybody held his breath. Then it stood up straight in the water, and began slowly, slowly to go down.

"He's getting there," said Quip, parenthetically, and referring, of course, not to Tom, but to the fish.

The last trace of the float was concealed by the water.

"Now pullJ" cried John.

Tom steadily and sturdily set about following this advice, but the something at the other end was pulling, too. For a moment the contest seemed equal. Then a shout of exultation broke from Tom as the line began slowly to yield.

"It's a whale or a shark," he muttered earnestly.

"Perhaps it'c the ghost of a water-logged Indian canoe," volunteered Keenan, who, like many boys under the first glad influence of poetic study, was seeking to develop his imagination at the expense of his friends.

"You might as well say it's the ghost of a shoe-factory," answered matter-of-fact Tom, indignantly.

Nearer and nearer came the end of the line. The water-hidden object of these speculations was acting very curiously, indeed. No jerking, no running away with the line, no leaping three or four feet out of the water after the manner of a game fish, no "sulking"—simply a strong, steady resistance.

"My opinion is, it's a mule," said Quip, solemnly.

"It must be a big log," said Keenan. "No game fish, not even a pumpkin-seed would conduct himself in that shabby manner. But keep

on.'

Tom needed no encouragement. Presently the cork appeared for a moment, but only to disappear again. The captive was now getting into shallow water.

"I see it!" shouted Ruthers.

"Can you see its ears?" asked Quip, consistent to his theory.

"It isn't a mule at all. It looks like a log."

"I see it, too!" cried Whyte a moment later. "It's round like a shield."

"My goodness, Tom!" continued Ruthers, "I

believe it's a turtle. But I never saw one so large before."

The last surmise was correct. An ugly, black head, with wide-open mouth, appeared above the water, followed soon after by a huge back fully eighteen inches in diameter.

"It's a snapping-turtle," said Donnel, u and the biggest one I ever saw."

The creature was now in very shallow water, and, with his feet more strongly braced, made prodigious efforts to escape. Donnel lent Tom a hand, and the King of the Lakes (we thank Keenan for this epithet) was soon landed.

But the struggle was not yet over. No sooner did he touch solid earth than he seemed to regain all his energies. He opened and shut his jaws with a vicious snap, accompanied this action with an angry hissing sound, and vainly tugged with his ugly forepaws at the hook fastened in his mouth. Tom, keeping the line taut, drew nearer him: the turtle faced his captor boldly 0

'Take care, Tom, he looks vicious," said Keenan. "Better kill him before you get too near him."

'Yes; but that's easier said than done."

"Look out, boys; clear the track," said Donnel, approaching with Tom's gun.

He took his stand over the turtle, and sent a charge into the creature which put an end to his ineffectual struggles.

"It weighs, I should judge, nearly fifty pounds," said Donnel.

u lt]s a great catch," added Keenan. "But snapping-turtles are no use for eating."

"Where's Percy?" cried Tom, looking around is he rose with the freed hook. Percy was nowhere to be seen.

CHAPTER VI

In which Percy Takes His First Lessons in Swimming and Rowing

U DERCY! Percy!" cried all.

"Here I am, boys," came a tremulous voice from above.

On raising their eyes, they were startled to discover Master Percy full fifteen feet from the ground, straddling the branch of a tree.

"How in the world did you get up there?" cried Harry.

"Really, I don't know; I wasn't aware I could climb a tree at all. But the fact is, whea that horrid turtle touched land—the nasty thing!— I found I could do almost anything."

The boys, who had been thus far gazing in astonishment upon Percy, now broke into a round, hearty laugh. Percy's confession was charmingly candid.

"It's all very well to laugh," said Percy, quite gravely, "but really my position is not at all comic. How am I going to get down? Oh, if my mamma were to see me, she'd faint!"

"One way would be to climb down," suggested Tom, dryly, and with the air of imparting valuable information.

: 'If you could wait for a while," Quip put in, "I'll £ ,and borrow an axe and bring you and tree ar i everything safe to the ground."

Percy's face gave no evidence of gratification at these wise proposals.

"Don't you think you could procure a ladder?" he asked anxiously.

This novel plan evoked a fresh burst of laughter.

u Oh dear, dear!" he groaned, "I was never in such an awkward plight in all my life." And his expressive lips began to quiver, and his eyes to grow dim.

John Donnel could not see a fellow-creature

in pain. The pathetic little face, now looking

i i • • i j- i

down upon him in deep dismay, was too much

for the big-hearted champion of the small yard.

"You're all right, Percy," he said. "J ust do what I tell you, and you'll be with us on solid ground without any more trouble than it would take you to walk down a flight of stairs. Simply place your feet on that branch below, and I'll attend to the rest."

Percy brightened at once—he had great confidence in John— and obeyed with alacrity.

u Now put your hands where your feet are, and let your feet drop. There, you're right as a trivet." And John, as he spoke, caught Percy around the ankles, and brought him gently to the ground.

"I'm not much of a boy," said Percy, humbly, "but I'll do better next time I see a snapping-turtle—I'll run away."

Fishing was now resumed in good earnest. Within an hour the party had caught a dozen large catfish, varying in weight from twelve ounces to a pound and a half. To the general mess Percy contributed eight small perch*

"Well," said Tom, looking at his watch, "It's about time for a swim."

"You don't mean to think of swimming here/" Percy exclaimed. 'Why not?" asked Tom.

"The turtles might snap at your legs. Ugh !" And Percy shivered.

"No danger of that at all, Percy," remarked Keenan. "Turtles don't go in much for boys' legs. They act on the principle, 'Live and let live.' "

"You're coming in too, Percy," added Tom, as though there were no choice in the matter.

"I! no, indeedy, — no, I won't!"

"But look," said Tom, impressively, and he produced from one of the baskets a pair of swimming-tights. "Here's a little present for you, Percy."

Instead of receiving it, Percy put his hands behind him, and backed away from the gift with a countenance expressive of anything but grati» fication.

"Well," said Tom, in disgust, "is that the way you receive a present ?"

Upon this, Percy, with whom politeness was almost an instinct, brought his face with a strong effort into a smile of gratitude. He advanced, and with a slight bow accepted the gift.

"Oh, thank you, Tom; they're ever so nice, Really," he continued, holding them up, and examining them with an approving eye, "they are quite beautiful. The stripes are nicer than a zebra's. I'll keep them in my desk at the college, Tom, and whenever I look at them I'll think of you."

This novel method of proposing to use a pair of swimming-tights did not suit Tom at all.

"Nonsense, Percy! they're not my photograph, I want you to use them. Swimming isn't so hard. It's much easier to swim than to climb

a tree."

Percy, it has already been observed, was most pleased in pleasing others. He saw that Tom was bent on his making a trial at swimming, and so, despite his fear of snapping-turtles, he submitted with the best grace possible.

Encouraged by Tom, he actually spent half an hour in the water, and was quite brave in his attempts to swim.

Percy had scarcely donned his garments, when, on turning his eyes out upon the lake, a cry of joy broke from his lips. A small row-boat steered by Quip and rowed by Keenan was making straight for the shore.

"Oh, do let me in with you, George!"

"What, go in a boat?" said Tom, banter-ingly. "Boats are dangerous. They upset so easily, you know."

"La! I'm not afraid," rejoined the reckless Percy. "I want to learn how to row."

"Jump in," said Keenan, as the boat's keel grated on the shore.

Percy took a seat along with George, who was in the middle.

"Now shove her off, Tom," said Quip.

Tom complied, and the boat shot out from the shore.

"Let me take an oar, George; I want to learn."

"I'll let you have both in a minute, Percy/ 1

George made answer; "but to begin with, you may try your hand at one. Now the very first thing you've got to learn is to keep stroke."

"Keep stroke? What with?"

"With your little hatchet, of course," remarked the grinning steersman, parenthetically.

"Don't mind that Quip; you keep stroke with your oar. The idea of keeping stroke is to draw back your oar, put it into the water, and pull at exactly the same time as I do it. The next thing you'll learn after that, I suppose, will be to catch a crab."

"Is it easy to catch a crab?" Percy innocently asked, as he made his first stroke.

"Easy as rolling off a log," interposed the irrepressible Quip, "and much in the same style, too.'

"How is it done ?" Percy continued as he bent back in making his third stroke.

"It comes natural," answered Quip, between bursts of laughter. 'You needn't try at all. You'll get there before you know it. You're sure to learn."

In taking his sixth stroke, Percy failed to dip his oar in the water, and suddenly toppled over backwards, his head, luckily for him, being caught by Harry Quip, who had been preparing for such an emergency, and his heels describing a series of rapid and irregular curves in the air. 'You've learnt it! you've learnt it!" shouted Quip, while George rested on his oar to indulge in a laugh. "That's just it; that's catching a crab. Now that you know it, you needn't practise it any more."

'Yes," said Keenan, helping Percy to his for-

mer position; "the practical application of knowing how to catch a crab consists in not doing it any more."

Percy, merrily laughing at his mishap, readjusted his cap, threw back his hair, and again set bravely to work with his oar. Considering that this was his first experience in a rowboat, he really acquitted himself with credit, and unconsciously he took his revenge on Harry Quip for his bravery. Like all beginners, Percy splashed water in every direction; and once when Harry had broken into a most hearty laugh at the beginner's awkwardness, Percy quite accidentally sent a jet of water flying into that young gentleman's wide-open mouth. The laugh was put out as though it had been a small conflagration.

When they sat down for dinner at one o'clock that afternoon, Donnel observed that Percy had developed a very pretty red rose on either cheek.

"It came from exercise," Keenan explained.

"And from becoming a boy, n added Tom.

"Yes," cried Percy, "that's just it. I'd rather be a boy than anything I know of. And oh, I'm so hungry! I never had such an appetite as far back as I can remember."

"Swimming always makes one hungry, and good cooking helps," said Harry Quip, who, having prepared the fish with great success, now strutted about bravely in a white apron, and with intense satisfaction watched the eatables disappear.

The afternoon passed happily; fish were caught in abundance. The homeward walk, too, .was delightful. Percy kept up his high spirits

to the end, and made the way pleasant with song, while, strange to say, he gave no sign of weariness.

"Well," he said, as they neared the college, "I'll have a grand letter to write to mamma and sister Mary. I'll tell them that I've learned to play leap-frog, to throw straight, to catch fish, to row a boat, to not catch a crab, and to swim on my back."

"They won't believe it all," said Donnel.

"Oh yes, they will," answered Percy. "They always believe whatever I say."

"There's one thing you're leaving out, Percy," said Tom soberly, "and it's the most important thing of the whole lot."

"What's that, Tom?"

"Tell your mamma youVe learned how to climb a tree."

In which Percy, Making way for the Heavy Villains of our Story, does not Appear

HERE was trouble brewing in the small yard. It came about in this wise.

About one month after the events narrated in our last chapter, Charlie Richards was endeavoring, as best he might, to enjoy the full holiday which the president of the college had given the students in honor of some local event. Accompanied by several of his companions, he had been moving restlessly about the yard, seeking for some amusement sufficiently exciting to raise his depressed spirits. Owing to previous misconduct, and especially to his cruel but unsuccessful attempt at playing ghost, he was not allowed to leave the premises; this privilege being given on recreation-days to those only whose general deportment afforded some assurance of their being trustworthy. But he was not alone in his enforced confinement. Nearly all of his chosen companions were under the same ban.

In the course of their aimless loitering here and there, they happened to come upon the wash-room. This apartment, except at certain appointed times during the day, was kept under lock and key. On this occasion, however, the door proved to be open. This fact aroused their curiosity. They entered. The only occupant was a slight child, who was engaged in black-

71

mg his shoes. His face, as Richards with his following made entrance, took on a look of dismay.

u Oh, please don't come in, boys," he said. "I forgot all about it. But Mr. Kane" (he was the associate prefect with Mr. Middleton), "told me to be sure and lock the door, and let no one in. It's all my fault; and if anything happens wrong, he'll blame me."

"Oh, it's you, Granger, is it?" remarked Richards, ignoring his request. 'You ought to be out walking; you're one of the good boys. What are you doing here?"

"I'm just getting ready to go up-town to meet my mother at the station. She's expected to come on the ten-o'clock train."

Richards was in bad humor, and, being in bad humor, the spirit of rebellion was stirring in his heart. He felt strongly inclined to do something contrary to rule.

"Well, clear out, Granger," he said. "I guess we can run this wash-room for a while, 5 '

"Oh, but I can't do that, Richards," answered poor Granger, who had a delicate conscience. "I must lock up the wash-room, and give the key back to Mr. Kane."

"Must you, indeed? You won't do any such thing. Come, now, clear out. Do you hear?"

"Well," said the little fellow, summoning all his resolution, "I'm going to do what I'm told. If you want to stay here, all right; but I've got to go now, and I'm going to lock the door after me. If you stay here, I'll have to lock you all

m."

"Indeed! You'll do nothing of the sort. 5

"Say, Richards," suggested John Sommers, "suppose we go out and lock him in?'*

Willie Granger, trembling but firm, walked as far as the door, and took the key from his pocket. With unsteady fingers he inserted it in the lock.

'Well, aren't you coming out?" he asked timidly.

By way of answer, Richards rudely pushed the child aside, hurriedly took the key from the lock and thrust it into his pocket.

His companions were already making themselves at home in the conquered territory. They were throwing about soap, combs, brushes, and other toilet articles, dousing each other with water, and indulging in such rude horse-play as among boys of coarser type is mistaken for fun.

Poor Willie Granger, looking on at this work of destruction, and divided between the anxiety of failing to meet his mother and the responsibility of leaving these boys masters of the washroom, burst into tears.

"Very well," he sobbed. "I'll go and tell Mr. Kane that I gave you the key. It's my duty."

"You will!" thundered Richards.

"Let's lock him in, and leave him here/' said Sommers, repeating his former suggestion,

"No," answered Richards, "we want the benefit of this room for ourselves."

"I have a better plan," said Peters. "Suppose we put him in the shoe-room?"

Beneath the stairs leading from the washroom to the dormitory was a small, dark apartment, employed for the keeping of shoes, base*

ball bats, foot-ball covers, and a variety of odds and ends.

When Granger heard this cruel suggestion, he saw that his only hope of safety was in flight.

But it was too late. The crafty Peters had already put himself between the door and his victim, and, as Granger made a burst for liberty, caught him securely round the waist.

Cruelty is contagious. Richards himself, under ordinary circumstances, would scarcely have taken pleasure in such conduct. But in his present ill-humor and his present company, the vile suggestion of Peters found ready entrance into his heart. It is hard, my dear reader, for us to be better than the company we keep.

Granger, upon being caught, gave a shriek of fear, and struggled with what frail strength he had to escape from his captor. But his endeavors were cut short, as Richards, Sommers, and a third member of the party caught him up, and proceeded to carry him over to the dark room; while another of this sorry band advanced to throw open the door.

In thorough terror, Willie Granger shrieked again and again. He was by no means a cowardly boy; still he was but a child —and children, unless of unusually steady nerves, cannot endure the idea of being shut up alone in the dark.

"Stop your yelling, will you?" threatened Richards, "or we'll gag you."

Even as Richards was speaking, Peters, disengaging his right hand, snatched a towel from one of the adjacent boxes, and forced it into Granger's mouth.

Suddenly Peters went spinning against the , and, as the towel fell from his hands, the water came to his eyes: to use the graphic school-boy expression, "he saw stars."

u You cowards!" ejaculated Tom Playfair, following up this blow to Peters with another upon Richards' chest, and with a third which sent Sommers toppling over an adjoining bench. "You cowards!"

Tom, brought to the scene cf action by Granger's cries of terror, had come upon them so quickly and unexpectedly that he had been able to make three of these "cowards" smart with pain, almost before they had become aware of his presence. But as Sommers went over the bench, several of the boys rushed upon Tom from behind, caught him tightly, and bore him to the ground. Tom, too, was in the toils.

The mad rage of Peters was something extraordinary. His face in an instant became livid with passion; he almost foamed at the mouth. Throwing himself upon Tom, who was held tightly to the floor, he was about to beat the unprotected face, when Sommers and Richards, who were somewhat cooler, interposed.

"Hold on," said Richards, pulling him forcibly off the prostrate boy, "we'll lock them both in."

Peters was constrained to agree.

But when they attempted to carry out their improved plan, fresh difficulties arose. For a boy of twelve, Tom was unusually strong: and he kicked and plunged with such effect, ^on^their attempting to raise him, that, besides inflicting minor injuries on several, he sent one of the

"cowards" doubled up and groaning into a corner. But the young villains were strong in their rage. Turning their attention to Granger, they easily succeeded in conveying him to the dark room; and leaving but one to guard him, all now lent a hand at subduing Tom.

"You're cowards, every one of you!" panted the struggling champion. "You're the meanest set that ever came to St. Maure's."

"Gag him! Tie him up! Bandage his eyes!" howled Peters, beside himself with passion.

They were about to carry out these vindictive suggestions, when the door of the play-room flew open, and a new face appeared upon the scene.

Tom was released instantly. Mr. Kane stood before them. The boys cowered under his eyes; their countenances changed from anger to fear, as they stood in shamefaced silence, expecting a great burst of indignation. But the prefect, standing in the doorway, said nothing. He simply gazed from one to the other, as if seeking to define from their faces the whole series of events.

Of all the boys, Tom was the only one who retained his composure in the least. Picking himself up, and calmly brushing his clothes, as though he were in the habit of being pulled about the floor of the wash-room by rude hands, he softly moved over to Willie Granger, who was standing near the door of the dark room, and in his kindest tones said:

"Here, Willie, take some candy."

For some time Mr. Kane continued to gaze on the terrified group; and as he stood silent second after second, his face gradually changed from its usual calm expression, not into anger, but into sadness.

"If I hadn't seen it," he said at length, and his voice trembled as though he were grieved almost to tears, "I could scarcely have believed the students of St. Maure's could go to such an extreme pass of cowardice. If I hadn't seen it, I could never have believed that their conduct would compare with the conduct of barbarians."

He paused for a moment: the sorrow upon his face to the culprits was worse than the most violent anger. With the exception of Peters, all were thoroughly and heartily ashamed.

"I never counted," he added presently, u on being obliged to deal with boys whose actions are suggestive rather of rowdyism than of Christianity. Go, now, Richards! go, all of you, except Playfair and Granger. As I am now, I am in no state to be able to decide clearly what punishment you should receive. I must have time to think."

"Did you say we were cowards?" asked Peters, sulkily, and making a vain endeavor to brazen it out.

"No matter what I said. It is certain that the vile attempt to persecute a defenseless child, and to lock him up in the dark, is the conduct of cowards; nay, it is more, it is the conduct of barbarians."

There was no tone of anger in Mr. Kane's voice; unaffected grief dominated the expression of all other feeling. Had he broken forth into violent rage, these delinquents might have put a bolder face upon their base conduct. But

this mode of taking them was novel and entirely unlooked-for. Crimsoning with shame, one by one they slunk from the room.

"Playfair," said Mr. Kane, changing his tone to one of genuine feeling, "I hope you're not hurt. You look as if you had been used rather roughly."

"Oh, I'm all right, sir," said Tom, cheerfully. "I got a little more exercise than I wanted, seeing as I intended to take a long walk this afternoon; but that's nothing."

'You're a good boy," said the prefect, heartily. 'Willie," he continued, turning to Granger, who was hardly yet over his fit of weeping, "you had better make haste if you wish to be on time for the train. You must brighten and brush up at once. Here, I'll help you."

Taking a clothes-brush, Mr. Kane kindly dusted the little victim's clothes, readjusted his tie, and then filled him a basin of water.

"Now wash the tears from your face, my boy. Your mamma would be pained to know that you've been crying. And you need have no fear of being molested by those boys a second time. This bullying must come to a stop."

"I don't think they're all bad fellows," said Tom, who had theories of his own on schoolboy life. "I believe that it's the crowd that is bad. Some of the fellows were good enough before they got together."

; 'I trust you are right, Playfair. Now, Willie," he added, turning to Granger, "if you start for the depot at once, you will easily make

it;

Willie Qranger, whose naturally bright and

happy face had already regained its usual expression, smiled gratefully.

"Thank you, Mr. Kane; I'm all right now, arid I'm sure mamma won't notice in the least that I've been in trouble. Good-by, sir."

And Granger set off for the depot in the best of spirits. The kindness of the prefect, and the heroic unselfishness of Playfair, contrasted with the cruelty of his persecutors, had given him new and exalted ideas of goodness. Even the doing of the wicked oftentimes serves to bring put more clearly the beauty of virtue. In an innocent and noble soul such a contrast may, at times and under proper conditions, develop a proper appreciation of what is really high and heroic.

When Tom issued from the wash-room into the yard he looked about for his recent foes. They were all clustered together in a corner of the hand-ball alley. With as much nonchalance as though nothing unusual had occurred between them, he walked straight into their midst.

"See here, boys," he said calmly. "I believe in being square, and I'm going to tell you just exactly what I think. You're all new fellows here, and I want you to know that most of the little boys of St. Maure's don't believe in bullying or imposing on the smallest chaps."

"Do you mean to say we're bullies, Tom Playfair?" asked Richards, menacingly.

"Why not?" answered Tom, blandly. "But just wait till I'm through talking. Now look here! The boys don't know much about you yet, and most of them haven't the least notion that you've been imposing on little chaps. You re-

member the day I caught you teasing Percy Wynn? Well, if I'd told some of the fellows about that, they'd have given you the cold shoulder. If I tell what's happened to-day, no decent boy in the yard will care about having anything to do with you. Now I don't intend to speak of it, so long as you behave properly. But as sure as I catch you at your mean tricks again, I'll publish you to the yard. Then you'll be cut dead."

"See here, Tom Playfair," said Peters, "do you want to fight?"

"Oh goodness, no ! I hate fighting."

"Are you afraid to try me?" said Peters, doubling up his fists, and growing braver in the face of Tom's tameness.

"Well, I am just a little afraid," admitted Tom.

'You're a mean coward," said Peters, "Come on, you blow-hard. I'm not afraid of a boy my

size.'

'That's just the difficulty," said Tom. 'You're not my size, you're ever so much smaller." [There was a difference between them of about three-fourths of an inch in Tom's favor.] "And besides, as I said, I'm afraid. You see, I might hurt you, and I'd feel very bad if I did. And even if you were as big as I am, I wouldn't fight, anyhow. Fighting is stupid, and, what's more, it's wrong."

Disregarding Peters' entreaties to "come on," Tom turned his back upon the crowd, and walked off with every sign of self-possession and security.

'The dirty little hypocrite!" hissed Peters.

V

"He's not such a bad fellow," said Richards,

•jvhose better nature was struggling to the surface. "I'm sure he was very honest and square in what he said."

u Yes," added Sommers. "I believe Play-fair is about right all through. We've been going wrong. I never felt meaner in all my life than when Mr. Kane was speaking to us about our bad conduct. The whole thing got to look so different when he appeared."

"Faugh! you milksop!" said Peters, wither-ingly, u do you want to desert us?"

"No— not that," answered Sommers, losing courage under the scornful glance and contemptuous words of Peters. 'We must all stick together, of course; but — but we might be a little more careful, I think, about not getting into trouble."

"That's it," Richards assented. "We'll enjoy ourselves, but try to keep clear of trouble, and especially not to get on the wrong side of Playfair. He's the most influential boy of his size in the yard. In fact, Donnel and Keenan are the only two who have more influence."

"Oh, so you're showing the white feather, too," said Peters, bitterly. "Indeed! Oh yes; you're quite right, so is Playfair, and we'll swallow everything Playfair says. Playfair said we're cowards — cowards!" repeated the wily villain. "And that's just what we're going to make ourselves. So we're going to let Mister Playfair go scot-free for getting us into trouble and then insulting us. He was right—we are cowards."

Peters had spoken like an accomplished

lain, as Indeed, considering his age, he certainly was. All writhed under his scathing words. One moment before, several of these boys had been on the point of choosing a better course; but they were cowards, not in Peters' sense of the word, however: they were not brave enough to withstand the sneers of one bad boy.

"See here, Peters," said Richards, his better nature again crushed under, "nobody said we were going to let Playfair abuse us without paying him back."

"Oh indeed! Then I'm badly mistaken; I thought that was what you meant."

'Well, I didn't say so, and I didn't mean any such thing either," retorted Richards, now bent on gaining the leadership which Peters was threatening to assume. "And what's more, I intend fixing that Playfair so that he'll remember he's insulted the wrong crowd to the last day of his life."

These words were enough. The current wa? turned back to the old channel. The last condition had become worse than the former. Revenge— low, brutal, unreasoning revenge—• found its way into the hearts of all. Peters smiled: he had brought things to the pass he desired.

"Good!" he exclaimed. "Richards, you're a trump. I don't know what your plan is for fixing Playfair; but if you have nothing to pro* pose, I've got an idea."

"Let's hear it," cried many, eagerly.

They drew closer together, and entered into a whispered conversation. Presently Sommers, who by his expression and gestures seemed to dissent from the proposed project, left the group and walked up and down the yard alone. He had deserted his comrades.

Mr. Middleton, who had entered the playground some five minutes after the affair in the wash-room, was now standing beside Mr. Kane at the other end of the yard, discussing with his co-laborer the morning's disgraceful event. While they continued their conversation, Mr. Middleton kept his eye upon the knot of boys, knowing with a prefect's divining instinct that their close and whispered interview could not be for good.

"Look!" said he, "keep a close watch on those boys. There's something in the wind. If we both be careful in connecting events today, by to-morrow probably we shall have a square case, and the crowd will go. It's the worst combination of little boys I have seen in St. Maure's since I've been here. It seems to me that there's an accomplished leader amongst them, and it is not Richards. If we find out the real leader, we can make short work of the rest."

"Don't you think Richards is the leader?" asked Mr. Kane. <T He is certainly the strongest, and generally seems to take the lead in everything."

"I thought so at first, Mr. Kane; but from little trifles I have noticed here and there of late, I have come to the conclusion that he is the figure-head. Somebody else is pulling the strings. But, please God, we'll know by tomorrow; for I see that things are coming to a head. The crowd has lost one member already.

Sommers is disgusted at something, and has cut away from them. It would be good to keep him out of harm's way for a while, and so give him no chance of weakening. Sommers," he called, as the lad, buried in thought, was passing by; "Sommers, come here one moment."

Sommers approached and raised his hat.

"Would you like to take a run up-town?"

The boy's eyes brightened. It was a privilege to go up-town; it became an honor when it embraced a confidential errand for the prefect.

"Certainly, sir."

"Very good. Here's a letter for the editor of the St. Maure's Express. When you give it to him, tell him you will return in an hour for the answer. In the meantime you may take a walk about the village, and amuse yourself as you please."

"Thank you, Mr. Middleton." And Sommers set forth brightly on his errand, his determination strengthened to give up for good and all his former company.

The prefect was a skilful judge of human nature in general, and of boy nature in particular. To one striving to rise from lower to higher nothing is so helpful, nothing so strengthening, as judicious and timely kindness. Probably, if Sommers had remained in the yard that morning, he would ultimately have been forced down by the pressure of human respect to his former level. But this kindly commission gave a new and lasting stimulus to his resolution. He was done with certain habits and associations forever.

His conversion, however, was not complete— .?t was not miraculous. Indeed, as he went on towards the village, there was a sharp, biting, fierce conflict between his awakened sense of duty and his human respect. He knew that a dastardly plan was preparing, which might result in serious harm to Tom Playfair; he knew, too, that one word from him might avert the danger. But the cost of that one word to him! the contempt of his former friends—their jeerings, their insults!

No: it was asking too much. He would take no hand in the matter, cost what it might. But for the rest, he would say nothing.

"Perhaps," he communed with himself, "something may spoil their plan. I hope so. But I haven't the heart to tell on my friends."

Not quite satisfied with himself, he kept his way towards the village, turning the matter in his mind, and vainly striving to square his resolution with his duty.

"Ah, I know what I'll do," he said, brightening. "If Tom doesn't come back to-night before bed-time, I'll tell."

This, after all, was but a compromise with his conscience: he could not but realize that it was his duty to give word at once, and so avert all danger.

But, in spite of his desire to do better, he was still a coward. Prayer and perseverance, let us hope, will in time give him true courage.

CHAPTER VIII In which Percy Makes a Desperate Resolve

IN THE meantime, we have been neglecting Percy. Where was he all the morning? Quietly seated at his desk in the study-hall. Too much exercise had again crippled him. So stiff and sore were his legs that it was with pain and difficulty he could move at all. Entirely ignorant, therefore, of the many events narrated in the last chapter, he read page after page of "Dion and the Sibyls." Nor did he leave the study-hall till the bell summoned him to dinner in the refectory.

The afternoon was inviting. The day had become warm and bright; so Percy, instead of returning to his desk, brought his book to the yard, and, desirous of avoiding all interruption, obtained permission from Mr. Middleton to retire from the playground proper into a little shaded recess beyond the old church-building. Here, selecting a cosy corner, he was soon wrapped in the story. Percy had the faculty of so concentrating his mind as to lose himself entirely in his reading — a fact which Tom Play-fair had been in the habit of verifying by picking Percy's pockets, filling them with stones, twisting his tie, and indulging in other such pleasantries, much to Percy's subsequent surprise. But on this afternoon no Tom Playfair was about to put his power of abstraction to the

test. All the same, Percy was far away from the land of the real. The shouts from the playground, the roaring of the passing train, the piping of the latest lingering birds, the occasional rumble of heavy wagons to and from St. Maure's,—these and a hundred other noises were entirely without the sphere of his consciousness. Several hours passed on. Percy was still in another land and dealing with other people.

Two boys stealing from the yard entered into earnest conversation almost within five feet of Percy, who was screened from their sight by a projecting end of the old building. As the conversation proceeded under his very ears (if I may use the expression), Percy did get an indistinct idea that he was not alone; but it was such an idea as one has in a dream, where, fully believing in the images presented by the fancy, one still realizes in a faint manner that one is not really awake. Hence the words of the two speakers fell upon ears that gave them no meaning. Had the boys then departed, Percy would never have been able to say positively that he had heard so much as one word.

Suddenly he was brought back from the days of Dion to his own little hour with a start; his book fell from his hand.

"Yes"—these were the words that attracted his attention — "Playfair may catch pneumonia, or something of the sort, if he's kept out all night in the frost and damp. It's almost sure to be cold to-night. I tell you, the thing is going too far. It's downright wicked—it's criminal!"

Percy recognized the voice as that of Som-

mers. "Well," said the other, whom Percy failed to make out, "it's too late now to do anything. Peters has found out some way or other — '-he seems to know everything—-that Quip and Playfair have taken an afternoon walk to Pawnee Creek. Peters and Richards and all the other fellows except you and me have gone walking with the prefect: and when the prefect stops to rest, they'll get permission to walk about for a while. Then they've arranged to get scattered from the other boys, and pretend, when they come home, that they've been lost. But just as soon as they get away from the old prefect's eyes, they're going to make for the old stone wall out on the prairie at a run. They'll fix a hiding-place there and wait till Playfair and Quip come along. Then they're going to tie and gag both of them, and if they can get a tree or post convenient they'll fasten them to

it."

UT'1

Til never have anything to do with those fellows again," said Sommers with energy. "Oh, I'm a coward! Why didn't I give a hint while there was time? But what's the use talking? If I had the morning over again, I'm sure I'd do the same thing. I am a coward. But what, on earth are they going to tie and gag Quip for?"

"Peters insisted on it. He says that Quip will be sure to smash the whole thing if he ence gets to the yard."

'Well, perhaps they won't catch them, anyhow," said Sommers. "Maybe Tom will walk home by the railroad-track."

"No, he won't. He's sure to come back along

by the place where they intend waiting for him Peters has found out in some queer way that the two intend to explore about Pawnee Creek till about four o'clock; then they are coming back, and, on the road, intend stopping to examine some rabbit-traps which they have set near the stone wall. Peters knows just where the traps are. He's a sharp fellow."

"I'm afraid there'll be some harm done," said Sommers, gloomily. 'Those fellows with Peters running them will be cruel as wild beasts. I feel that Peters has made me act that way more than once. They'll tie those poor boys so tight that they'll not be able to move a limb, and, besides the danger of passing a night in the cold, they'll be sore for weeks. Well, it can't be helped, I suppose."

Imagine Percy's terror and anxiety on hearing these words! His best friend in danger! What could he do? Here he was, unable to walk one step without pain—and Tom and Harry separated from him by several miles!

"O my God!" murmured Percy, "give me light, give me grace, give me grace." Percy had the beautiful habit of having recourse to God in all dangers and difficulties. With him prayer was a living thing, not a formality.

For several minutes he prayed and pondered, pondered and prayed; while, in the meantime, the two boys had again slipped into the yard. Finally, throwing his books to one side, he hurried, despite his stiffness, into the playground, and looked anxiously around. Only a few boys were about, none of whom he could take for a friend in counsel.

"Oh, if I could just find Donnel or Keenan!" thought Percy. "Oh, Mr. Middleton!" he said, addressing the prefect, "can you tell me where I might find John Donnel or George Keenan?"

"They're out walking, Percy," answered Mr. Middleton, who perceived at once that the boy was in a state of unusual excitement, "and they won't be back in all probability till supper-time. It is now a little after three. What's the matter, my boy? you look troubled."

Percy stood in thought for a moment before replying. Like most students he hated anything in the nature of tale-bearing, especially if the matter could be settled without bringing his school-fellows into trouble with the authorities. It had been his intention to inform Keenan and Donnel of the state of affairs as he understood it, trusting to their tact and energy to bring Tom and Harry through unharmed. Would it be wise, he pondered, to tell the prefect? After all, he himself might set out, warn Tom, and thus avert the impending danger, without ex* posing his fellow-students to punishment. Be* sides, he felt that he could scarcely make a straight story out of what he had gleaned from the conversation. Here and there he had lost a word; and all that he could clearly make out was, that if Tom and Harry were to return home by the road they had resolved upon, across the prairies, they incurred the danger of spending the night bound and gagged in the open air. In a moment he had made his resolve. He himself, without informing Mr. Middleton of what was on foot, would defeat the plan.

Perhaps it had been wiser had Percy told all that he knew to the prefect. In grave cases it often becomes a duty to inform higher authorities. But he acted according to his lights. Had he realized that it was proper and right for him to reveal the scheme, he would certainly have done so. But on this occasion there was no time for the balancing of nice probabilities.

"Mr. Middleton, would you please give me permission to go out and meet Tom and Harry? I have something very important that I want to tell them."

The prefect was wondrously sympathetic with boy-feelings. He perceived at once that Percy had strong reasons for preferring his request. But being a very considerate man touching school-boy honor, he refrained from worrying the lad with further inquiries. And yet a fine instinct in regard to the thoughts and emotions of students does not necessarily supply information as to their state of physical health. Had Mr. Middleton but known how stiff and sore were poor Percy's legs, he might have taken a different course.

"Yes, you may go."

"Oh, thank you, Mr. Middleton! I shall never forget your kindness. Could you please tell me the shortest way to Pawnee Creek?"

"The shortest way is across the prairie; the surest, along the railroad. But have you ever been there?"

"No, sir, but I know the direction." And Percy waved his hand so as to embrace the whole east in a general way.

"Don't trust the prairie, then: those undula-

tions are very deceptive. Before you know it, you'll be lost, and after an hour's walking you may find that you've been going in a circle. Better take the railroad-track. It's' a good four miles, and will take you at least an hour's sharp walking."

"Oh dear! oh dear!" almost groaned Percy, "and it's three o'clock now."

"Just ten minutes past three."

"Well, good-by, sir." And Percy, realizing that not one moment was to be lost, made his polite little bow, turned and walked rapidly towards the gate leading from the yard.

His kind, affectionate heart was throbbing with suspense. What if he should miss them? What if they were to resume their homeward route earlier than four o'clock?

As he reached the gate, he heard his name called. He turned, and discovered Mr. Middleton hurriedly advancing towards him.

"Hold on one moment, Percy," said the prefect, who had evidently been pursuing some similar train of thought. "I've been thinking you may have some difficulty in finding your friends. Here is a whistle which may be of some use to you. It makes a tremendous noise, and carries to a good distance. You might try it, if you can't get sight of Tom and Harry."

"Well, if you aren't just too kind!" exclaimed Percy, his round, blue eyes and mobile lips expressing the liveliest gratitude. "Mr. Middle-ton, I'll love you and pray for you the longest day I live."

And with a smile and a bow, he hurried away, leaving the good prefect buried in thought.

which Percy Makes a Brave Fight Against Discouragements

on the railroad-track, and beyond sight of the yard, Percy broke into a run. Under the excitement of the occasion, he no longer felt the stiffness in his limbs. No one looking at him now would imagine that but a few hours before he could scarcely move across the yard, For several minutes he trotted sturdily on, the quick patter of his feet being the only noise to disturb the silence; till, by degrees, his breathing, growing shorter and shorter, also lent its aid towards disturbing the solemn stillness, But he continued to hold his pace, though at every moment he panted more and more. Finally his heart began beating so violently that he became frightened.

"Oh dear, dear! What shall I do?" he murmured as he relaxed his pace to a walk. "I'm so weak and short-winded, and poor Tom and Harry in danger. Oh, my dear angel, help me!"

For five or six minutes he walked briskly on, — almost every step accompanied by an ejaculation to his invisible guide for help — till he came to a mile-stone.

"One mile passed. Only three miles more. Now for another spurt."

With a yet more earnest prayer to his attendant angel, whom, like a Catholic boy, he

really saw with the vision of trusting faith, he again broke into a run. But this time he gave out much sooner. In less than four minutes he was going at a walk. To add to his trouble and anxiety, the morning's stiffness reasserted itself. Every step was now registered in pain, and his pretty, delicate face was flushed with exertion and beaded with sweat. But his compressed lips and his steady eye gave evidence that in that poor, pain-racked frame there dwelt the spirit and the will of a hero. Did I say that every step was registered in pain? Doubtless every step was also registered in a place where pain and sorrow enter not, but where love and peace and rest are forever.

The torture increased as he went on, till the tears came to his eyes. They came, and coursed down his cheeks. But it would be useless to turn back. No one but himself could now carry out the work of warning Tom and Harry, And yet he felt the strongest of desires to throw himself down on the earth, and simply lie there. How inviting the withered autumn grass beside the track appeared to his dimmed eyes!

"Oh dear, dear!" he thought. "Surely I'm giving out. But if I give up, poor Tom and Harry will—But I won't give up. No, I'll walk right on; and I'll not stop so long as I'm able to move."

But notwithstanding the firmness of his resolve, groan after groan broke from his lips.

"Hurrah!" he faltered presently, "there's the second mile-stone."

As he spoke, a sudden and strong gust of wind from the north came upon him, carrying away his hat. But of this little misfortune he took no notice. What was his hat to him now? But Tom and Harry! He again broke into a run.

Strange to say, he held his pace much longer this time than even in his first attempt. But his delicate features had become knotted with pain; his long, golden hair, the sport and plaything of the unfeeling wind, had become all dishevelled, throwing itself about his eyes, or floating wildly in the breeze. Poor child! Who, looking at him now, would have recognized in him the "mamma's darling" of the last month? In that frail, delicate body there dwelt a brave heart.

For some seven or eight minutes, he had been running briskly along, when he happened to strike his foot against one of the railroad-ties. He stumbled and fell prone. A dizziness came upon him, a strong, blind, unreasoning desire to stay where he fell, to lie there and rest—rest, come what might. His head fell back; his eyes closed. A stupor was upon him. Tom and Harry's case seemed lost. A moment passed, and with a shiver his eyes opened again and consciousness returned.

"Help me. Mother Mary!" he moaned.

With a strong effort of the will, he arose and resumed his walk, his head still swimming, his heart beating more violently than ever, literally thumping against his ribs; but on he pressed,

Presently a sound— it was not a cry—of joy broke from his parched lips. The bridge — Pawnee Bridge—was in sight; far off, but still in sight.

"Oh, thank God! thank God!" he said, OF rather attempted to say, for his cracked and parched lips refused to do their duty.

Alternately walking and running, he made forward with revived energy. Nearer and nearer came the bridge. Hope grew stronger, and supplied the place of physical strength. One spurt more, but a few hundred yards, and the bridge spanning Pawnee Creek would be gained.

There he was at length, panting, breathless, his hat gone, his clothes covered with dirt and dust; his unprotected hair all dishevelled, his face twisted with pain; yet triumphant in hope, there he was, leaning against the side of the bridge, his eyes scanning the country roundabout on all sides. Alas! no sight of Tom or Harry! He drew the whistle from his pocket, and put it to his lips. It gave a high, penetrating sound.

But what should he do now ? Were it best to wait for a possible answer to the call, or should he move along Pawnee Creek? He decided to explore further. But here a new difficulty presented itself. The creek flowed towards the river. Should he trace its course to its mouth, or rather should he go up-stream along its windings through the prairie? He was entirely ignorant of the locality; but reflecting that Tom and Harry were to take the prairie on their way back to college, he quickly decided to go upstream. Almost dragging himself, he moved with labored steps towards an eminence several hundred yards off on the prairie, which, he judged, would command an extensive view of the creek in its various windings. It was an agonizing progress, but love and hope spurred

him on, in spite of growing languor, in spite of increasing weakness, in spite of a thousand sharp pains. Half-way up the eminence, he was compelled to stop from sheer exhaustion; his head seemed to be turning round and round; he felt that he was about to fall.

"Heart of Jesus," he murmured, "strengthen me !"

Percy believed in prayer; hence his prayers were never unheard. He again pressed on. A few painful, toilsome moments and the summit was gained. In part his expectations were realized. The eminence did command an extensive view of the stream; for over half a mile he could descry its various nooks and bends, except where the trees lining its banks were unusually thick. But no sight of the two boys.

Percy did not burst into tears. His sufferings were too deep for such expression of grief, but his heart grew sick. Again he swept the horizon. Half a mile from the creek, in a westerly direction, arose a prairie undulation of unusual size. Were there not two figures in it, standing out in the light of the dropping sun? Percy could not make sure. His head was still swimming, and a mist was before his eyes. Yes, surely there must be something there; could it be they? But even so, they were beyond his calL He was powerless to catch their attention. What could he do? Oh yes, the whistle. Once more he blew it, clear and loud. Was it heard? Were the figures he perceived merely an illusion of the fancy or really his two friends? And did they, as it seemed to him, turn at the sound. He was sure of nothing; but he again blew the

whistle, and made a great effort to shout. Poor fellow! his cry would not have disturbed a singing bird at his side.

His dizziness increased; scarcely knowing what he did, he eagerly looked about him. At his feet there chanced to lie a long pole— doubtless once used by some St. Maure students on a fishing excursion. Hastily tying his handkerchief to its tapering end, he raised the rod into the air and waved it several times; then staggered and fell to the earth senseless.

CHAPTER X

In Which Percy Rescues Tom and Harry; Tom

and Harry Rescue Percy; and a Third

Party Rescues the Trio

* PERCY, old fellow, don't you know me?" Tom, supporting Percy's head upon his bended knee, was looking down earnestly into the child's face.

Percy, who had just opened his eyes, smiled with a great joy.

'Water," he whispered.

"Hurry up, Harry!" shouted Tom, turning his head towards the creek.

Harry came breathlessly up the hill with a tin can filled with water. Percy drank of it eagerly; the color returned to his pallid face.

"That's right, old boy," said Tom. "You'll be as good as new in a minute."

"Oh, Tom," said Percy, pressing his hand, "I came so near missing you."

"I should rather say you did. If it weren't for the infernal noise you made with that whistle, Harry and I would have been halfway back to St. Maure's by this time. But what on earth brought you out here, losing yourself tramping over the prairie, when any sensible boy with legs like yours would be in bed? Suppose you had missed us in the state you are in now; you mightn't have been able to get home tonight. But I suppose something must have gone wrong. Has anybody been bothering you?"

"Oh, no, Tom, the boys as a rule are very kind to me. And when they do tease me for being just a little too girlish, you know, they are so good-natured about it."

u Oh, awfully!" said Tom, sarcastically.

"I came," continued Percy, "to tell you both not to go home the way you intended, but to take the railroad-track."

whistled.

r ou don't mean to say," he exclaimed, "that you've nearly ruined your little legs, and half killed yourself, to come and tell us another way of walking home!"

'Yes, Tom. If you go home the way you intended, there's Richards and a lot of others-— Peters, and I don't know who else—who are in hiding by this time, waiting to tie and gag you, and leave you out on the prairie all night. I was so afraid I wouldn't find you two; and I did come very near missing you; but now I'm perfectly happy.

For the first time in a long while, Tom's eyes filled. Harry Quip fairly cried.

"Well, Percy Wynn, if ever I said you weren't a real boy, I was a fool," said Tom, in a tone wherein energy and feeling were equally blended. "You couldn't walk a single foot without pain when I left you after dinner; and now you come four miles to help a poor idiot like me. YouVe almost killed yourself for us two. Oh, Harry!"

And Tom furtively wiped his eyes. 'Dear me!" said Percy, "please, please don't make such a fuss about it. It really wasn't so very hard, and Fm not hurt in the least. It's

only because I can't stand much exercise that I gave out. Indeed, I'd gladly do much more for either of you."

"I know what a boy is now better than ever I did before," pursued Tom. "I thought I knew a lot yesterday; but now I feel as ignorant as a young calf. Oh, Percy, how could you?"

Percy arose.

"Come on, boys. I'm all right, and we can start for the college now. And really, I never was so glad in all my life. You see, I didn't hope ever to be of any use to you."

"But you are, and you were," protested Tom. "And you've taught me more than all my books."

"And I never expected you'd teach me half as much as you've done this hour, Percy," added Harry, whose emotion had sufficiently subsided to allow him to put his gratitude into words; "though, all along, you've made me do a heap of thinking, since I first met you."

These two friends were beside themselves with admiration at Percy's noble and self-sacrificing conduct. Justly to appreciate nobility, one must be noble one's self.

"But how are we going to get back?" asked Harry. "You could hardly bring yourself this far, and you've nearly the same distance to go over again."

"Oh, I think I can walk," said Percy, bravely. "It was the running which wore me out. I had less than an hour to make it in."

In silence they moved slowly towards the railroad-track.

"Oh," said Tom t clinching his fists indig-

nantly, "if Keenan or Donnel were with us, you may be sure we'd go back the way we intended."

"It's growing colder," added Harry, reflectively, "and we're going to have a frosty night. Ugh! just think of shivering out here in the Kansas gentle zephyr, and not being able to move, or say as much as 'Howd'y' do' ?"

As they wended their way slowly college-wards, Percy told them how he had happened to overhear the plot against them; but his voice was extremely weak, and Tom noticed with anxiety that his steps were faltering, and at times lines of pain revealed themselves on his face.

It was now getting on towards five o'clock, and they had accomplished barely half a mile.

"Percy," said Tom, when the boy had made an end to his narration, "you're not fit to walk. You mustn't do it. Oh, I'd give^ anything if I could lend you my legs; they'd be in decent company for the first time."

"Don't mind me, Tom; I'm all right. Of course, I am a little stiff, you know. I've never had any practice at running."

"Well," said Tom, "Harry and I will lend you as much of our legs as we can. Here, Harry, get his right arm and brace him up. I'll *ake the other. Let's imagine we're policemen, and that we're hustling this young man off to the station."

"I wish we were policemen," said Harry as he complied with the suggestion. "Wouldn't I whistle and yell for a patrol-wagon? Oh no!"

Thus supported, Percy went on for a long time. But in spite of their assistance, his anxious friends noticed that the ghastly pallor was

deepening on his face, and that sharp spasms of pain were ever and anon racking his delicate frame.

"And all this for me and Harry," Tom reflected, his eyes again filling. "If we don't do something, the boy will be ruined for life. I wish he hadn't heard of that plot. Even if 7 didn't manage to scratch through, I'd rather spend a week bound and tied than see poor Percy in such a state." He added aloud: "Here, let's stop one moment and take a rest."

There was a grass-covered embankment hard by, which at once suggested itself for a stopping-place.

Tom and Harry instinctively threw off their coats and silently arranged them as a temporary mattress for the sufferer.

"Now, Percy," added Tom in his gentlest tones, as he seated himself, "lie down on these coats: you're so heated from your exertions that you'll surely catch cold if you lie on the ground. I'm sorry there's nothing like a pillow convenient, but you must make the best of my knees."

Percy smiled affectionately on Tom as he obeyed the order. He sank back, and almost immediately his eyes closed as though he were lost to consciousness.

Both boys gazed in lively anxiety on the still, calm, beautiful face. They were in the great-est alarm. To them that face was as the face of the dead.

"Harry," said Tom after a few moments of thinking, and his voice had sunk to a grave whisper, "it's nonsense to think of Percy's taking another step. I'll stay with him here for a while, and then I'll try to carry him along tHc track, (oh, if I were a man for an hour or so!) and you had better start right now, and run as hard as you can till you get off to the town-road crossing the track, and try to get some wagoner to wait and give us a lift. I'll be on as soon as I can."

Without delay or hesitation, Harry set off at the pace of a foot-racer. He was an excellent runner, and with the skill of long practice, he had no doubt that he would reach the road—a little over a mile off—within seven or eight minutes.

Presently Percy's eyes opened.

"Oh, Percy!" cried Tom. "Thank God! How are you now, old boy? Don't you feel better?"/

The invalid noticed Tom's anxiety and alarm

"Oh, yes, mdeedy!" he said with a bright smile. "I think I can go on now." 'Very good, Percy. On you go."

Percy was in too weak a condition to express his surprise at the extreme novelty of the proceedings, when Tom, as if it were but a matter of every-day life, picked him up in his arms and started off for the college.

Luckily for Tom, Percy, though a year older, was very lightly built. Still he was an extraordinary weight for a boy of twelve to carry. Tom, however, was strong and enduring. Gratitude, too, and generosity came to his aid.

So onwards he moved with quick and steady stride, his countenance, though he could not but breathe heavily, fixed into a matter-of-fact expression, as though the work in hand were some-

thing he had given himself to from early youth. Percy said nothing; but his face expressed wonder.

"Don't be alarmed, Percy; Fm not tiring myself one bit," he said reassuringly. "In fact, I rather enjoy it: I'm awfully fond of exercise, you know. I'd run with you, only I'm afraid of tripping up."

Suddenly Tom perceived through the gathering darkness a horseman coming towards them at a furious gallop. His heart beat high with hope as horse and rider drew nearer and nearer.

"Hurrah!" he said as the approaching help within the distance of his distinct vision.

"Well ! did you ever hear of such a thing, Percy? If it isn't Mr. Middleton!"

CHAPTER XI

In Which Mr. Middleton Finds His Lost Sheep, Both White and Black

M

R. MIDDLETON it was. A few words will explain his presence.

When Mr. Kane had returned about supper-time from his walk, and reported Richards, Peters, and some seven or eight others absent, a light dawned upon Mr. Middleton's mind. H* remembered distinctly the morning's incidents; he called to mind Percy's anxiety to meet Tom and Harry. Clearly there was some evil scheme on foot, which Percy had set out to frustrate.

"Mr. Kane," he said hurriedly, "will you please take the boys to supper this evening? I must make an examination into this matter at once; I fear there is something wrong going on."

Girding up his habit, he hurried over to the stables back of the college, saddled the swiftest horse, and set out with all speed for Pawnee Creek.

As his horse trotted on over the prairie, the prefect's watchful eyes caught sight of a skulking figure hastily retreating under shelter of the old stone wall. Putting spurs to his horse, he came a moment later upon the conspirators all huddled together. With a prefect's practised glance, he took them in. Every one of Mr. Kane's reported absentees was there.

"Go home at once," he said sternly. "It is now twenty minutes before supper-time. If a single one of you report late, his case will become even more serious than it is now."

Leaving the disconcerted band in a state of terror, he now took his way at more leisure, always contriving to keep the railroad in sight.

Some few minutes later, the prefect from an eminence on the prairie perceived some one running at full speed along the track. In an instant he was upon him.

"Oh, Mr. Middleton," shouted Harry, "I'm just looking for help. Poor Percy is about half-dead. You'll find him and Tom about a mile farther down the track."

"Why didn't you take him home the shorter way across the prairies, if he was so weak?" asked the prefect, hurriedly.

"Because—because Percy didn't want us to take that direction," answered Harry, evasively.

"Hum ! Take a rest here, Harry, and try to get your breath before I send Tom on to join you. I'll take care of Percy."

He dashed on with increased speed, till he came upon Tom, now walking rather unsteadily under his delicate burden.

"Good boy, Tom! good boy! But you are worn out. Is Percy unconscious?"

"Oh, Fm all right, Mr. Middleton. How do you do, sir?" answered Percy in a faint voice. "Only my legs are a trifle weak."

"Can you hand him up to me, Tom?"

"Certainly, «ir," said the young porter, puffing at a great rate. "He's not as bad as some dumbbells I've lifted."

Mr. Middleton placed Percy in front of him, as conveniently as the circumstances would pep-mit.

"Poor child!" he said sorrowfully. "It's all my fault, too. I should have remembered, when you spoke to me this afternoon, that you were in no condition to walk."

"Oh, I'm so glad you let me go, Mr. Middle-ton ! I wouldn't have missed that walk for anything."

"Well, Tom," continued the prefect, "push on along the track; you'll find Harry, who is as much out of breath as yourself, awaiting you. Percy and I will go on ahead, and we'll manage to have a good supper ready for both of you; won't we, Percy?"

Percy smiled faintly.

'When you reach the college, go straight to the infirmary, —you and Harry. I'll persuade the infirmarian to have supper for three, and an extra one at that."

Mr. Middleton then turned the horse's head and, at a pace suitable to the delicate condition of his companion, made for the college. He drew rein at the door of the infirmary, and, descending with his charge, entered the small boys' sick-room.

"Brother, here's a boy who tried to see how far he could walk without killing himself," he said to the infirmarian, as he gently laid Percy on a bed. "He's very weak, as you see, and needs something to tone him up."

The Brother hurried into the little drug-shop hard by, and quickly returned with a small glass of light wine.

"Swallow that, boy, and you'll feel ever so much better at once. I'm glad you've come," he continued as Percy emptied the glass, "for there's not a boy in the infirmary at present and I'm so anxious for something to do that I've begun to feel lonesome."

"Oh, by the way," said Mr. Middleton, "you won't be so lonesome to-night, I fancy. There are two more boys, Playfair and Quip, whom I have ordered to come here. They'll be on very soon. Both of them have had a rather hard time of it helping Percy on; and as they are very tired and too late for supper, I'm sure you'll be kind enough to give them board and lodging for the night in your best style."

"That I will," said the Brother, heartily, and rubbing his hands. "They'll get such a supper to-night as they never yet had in St. Maure's."

"Excellent! Now I've quite a number of things to clear up, if possible, before night-studies begin; so I'll leave everything to you. Good-by, Percy."

"Good-by, Mr. Middleton. My sisters, no, not even my mamma, could have been any kinder to me than you have been."

The prefect smiled as he hurried out. I suspect that his haste was partly caused by the fear of being discovered in the act of blushing.

The boys had finished supper some time before, and were now engaged at play, preparatory to night-studies. But Mr. Middleton, instead of going to the yard, returned to his room, sending word through a student, whom he chanced to meet in the corridors of the main building, that he wished to see Richards*

PERCY WYNN

Seating himself at his desk, the prefect buried his face in his hands, and surrendered himself to a train of thinking.

"I'm going to find all the ins-and-outs of this matter the reflected. "Let us put together what I know. Playfair interfered with these fellows this morning, when they set upon persecuting little Granger; and, owing to Mr. Kane's appearance on the scene, they come off worst. Then they hold some evil counsel in the yard. Whatever it is, it is something more than usually bad; for Sommers leaves them. Ah! by the way, Sommers did not go out with them on the walk. Then Percy came on the scene, all f ngh' and anxiety, having evidently got some word of their machinations. He goes out to warn Tom and Harry. The conspirators don't return with their companions from the walk. I go out, and discover them all in hiding beside the stone wall. It seems clear enough that they expected Tom and Harry to return from the creek in that direction; it is clear, too, that their scheme, whatever it was, was to be carried out there; and lastly, it is no less clear that Tom and Harry, who know the walks well, would surely have come back that way had they not been warned, for it is by far the shortest and most pleasant road. Now the great question is, what were the intentions of these boys in endeavoring to waylay Tom? And, more important still, who is the real ringleader? However, there'll be little difficulty, I believe, towards getting something definite on both these points."

He had scarcely pieced out these circumstances, when there came a knock at the door.

"Come in."

Richards, crestfallen, pale, and trembling, entered.

'Well, sir. This is a pretty business. I believe Mr. Kane told you and your sorry companions this morning that you were acting like cowards. I fear that he rather understated the real fact. What have you to say for yourself, sir?"

"Really, sir, and truly, I didn't propose the plan," protested Richards. "I'm awfully ashamed of the whole matter; I am, upon my word, sir. Oh, Mr. Middleton, it never oc< curred to me, when I first agreed to the thing, that it would turn out to be a frosty night."

"Oho! exposure to the night air," thought the prefect; "that's something." He added aloud: "But you should have thought of it. Suppose the boys were to have contracted some grave malady from exposure?"

"Well, I objected all along to tying them and gagging them; but Peters said they'd make such a noise as to spoil everything."

"Oh, indeed!" said the prefect, who now knew all he desired. "I'll consider the case. You may go."

"But, Mr. Middleton, upon my solemn word, I'll change if you give me another chance. Indeed I will. Please don't get me expelled this time. I am sure I can do better. I never thought I should go so far. I'll have nothing to do with Peters after this; and you'll see that I'll act quite differently."

"Well," answered Mr. Middleton, really moved by the lad's sorrow and distress, "I'll try to save you, Charlie; to-morrow we'll have a talk together, and I'll give you some advice."

"Thank you, sir. I'll do anything you think proper."

"I thought so," reflected the prefect, as Richards left the room; "Peters is the real leaden

Richards is his cat's paw. Peters must have caused these boys to believe that, on account of the large number concerned, there would be no thought of expulsion. Still he must assuredly! have a strong hold on them to bring them round to so hare-brained a scheme. Certainly he is a dangerous boy. No enterprise so hazardous and wicked has come under my notice since my coming to St. Maure's."

Meanwhile, the party in the infirmary were having, as Harry Quip styled it, "a high old time." Tom and Harry, to do them justice, had capital appetites after their long excursion; and the service was indeed, as the Brother had promised, something extraordinary. How the buttered toast did disappear ! and the eggs ! and the jam ! Well, I shall say nothing on that matter, lest the gentle reader may think I wish to slander the young trio.

The good infirmarian compelled Tom to tell the whole story over again —he had heard it already from Percy —and then called upon Quip to narrate it, which that young gentleman did with some interpolations very creditable to his imagination, but very astonishing to his hearers, who were kept quite busy contradicting him and keeping him down to facts. The Brother's delight knew no bounds. (

"It's as good as a book," he said, rubbing his

hands. "If I had time, I'd write it out and pub-

i • * • • • i

iish it."

Harry Quip was in great form on this memorable evening. He told funny stories until the room rang with laughter—Percy's sweet, silvery voice above the rest. Our little hero was too weak to do the meal justice, although Tom and Harry more than supplied his deficiencies in this respect. But how he did laugh! In spite of his aching limbs, he beamed with joy. When, at length, the conversation began to flag, nothing would do him but to sing a song.

"Aren't you too tired to sing?" queried Tom.

"Oh la! no. It refreshes me to sing."

"And it makes me infinitely weary," said Harry, with an eye twinkling the contradiction to his words.

'Well, here's something in honor of our host, the Brother." And Percy, with much feeling, gave Moore's beautiful "Harp that once through Tara's Halls."

The effect upon the infirmarian was marked. As he listened, his old eyes kindled with enthusiasm till they became dimmed with tears.

"Are you from Ireland, boy?" he asked, when Percy's voice had ceased.

"Not directly, 5 ' answered Percy. ; I've come most of the way, though. I'm from Baltimore; but my mamma comes from there."

"Well," said the enthusiastic Brother, "1 didn't think any one away from the old sod could sing like that."

The talking and laughing resumed right merrily.

"Boys," said Percy, when the hour-hand of

the clock was hard upon the number nine, "do you know I think this is a punishment to my vanity."

"What?" asked Quip, innocently. u The supper?"

"Of course not, you tease! I mean my sore legs."

"How's that ?" asked Tom.

'Well, you know I used to dance a great deal with my sisters, and I was very vain of my skill. But," he added ruefully, u now I'll never be vain of my legs again."

"After that remark," said the Brother, "I think you had all better go to bed."

Meantime, the small boys were poring over their books in the study-hall. The study-keeper noticed, as he took his seat, which commanded a view of the whole room, that the students were restless; and although he had heard nothing of the late events, he at once inferred that something out of the common had happened.

On running his eyes down the benches, he perceived that there were several vacant seats; and taking out the "map" of the study-hall, h« set about ascertaining the names of the absentees.

He was about to make a note of the missing ones, when Mr. Middleton quietly entered, and advancing noiselessly up the aisle, whispered in his ear:

"Is Martin Peters here?"

"No," said the study-keeper ; "there's his seat, second bench on the second row."

Peters had run away.

CHAPTER XII

In Which Mr. Middleton Makes a Discovery^ and Passes a Restless Night

'HEN Charlie Richards left Mr. Middle-ton's room, he was a changed boy. He realized that his course thus far at college had been the downward course, and, reflecting bitterly on the events of the day, he was appalled at the depths to which he had descended.

As he reached the foot of the stairs, he noticed that the study-hall was open, and, desiring to avoid the boys for the present, he entered.

As his foot crossed the threshold, he was roused from his thoughts by the slamming of a desk. He raised his head, and found that he was face to face with Martin Peters, who, standing by the side of Percy Wynn's desk, looked very much out of countenance.

"I was just hunting for my Latin grammar," said Peters, speaking hurriedly. "Some fellow has stolen it."

"Peters," said Richards, "I'm sorry for you. I didn't mean to tell, but I was so frightened just now, when I was talking with Mr. Middle-ton, that I rather think I let him know you were at the bottom of this dirty business. I'm sorry that I've got you into trouble; at the same time, I'm more sorry that I ever allowed you to run me. I've been a fool."

"Well," said Peters, in a voice strange and

forced, "I guess I'll look for that Latin grammar during studies." And with an expression on his face which, in the light of after-circumstances, Richards never forgotj Peters hurried from the study-hall.

At studies that night Charlie noticed Peters' absence at once, and, as his strange manner and remarks about the loss of the Latin grammar recurred, a horrible suspicion flashed upon his mind.

Whilst he was still under the influence of this horrible suspicion, Mr. Middleton, whom he had seen enter the study-hall and speak with the study-keeper, advanced to his side.

"Richards," he whispered, "do you know anything about Peters?"

"No, sir. Just after leaving your room I came in here, and saw Peters, He said he was looking for his Latin grammar, and that some one had stolen it."

"Was he looking for it iff the desks?" continued Mr. Middleton.

"Yes, sir; at least I think he was. When I came in he was closing one."

Mr. Middleton advanced on tiptoe to Peters' desk, threw the cover up, and glanced over the books.

Peters' Latin grammar was there.

Mr. Middleton's face remained unchanged, he knew that nearly every eye in the study-hall was fastened on him.

He returned to Richards' place.

"What desk was he closing when you entered the room?"

"Percy Wynn's, sir."

'Very good. Now, my boy, please go outside the study-hall, and wait for me in the passage, as I shall probably have something to say to you. You needn't be alarmed, Charlie," he added in a kindly voice, as he noticed the expression of uneasiness which came upon Richards at these words. "I have spoken to the president about your case, and all will be well."

As Richards left the study-hall, the prefect moved softly over to Percy's desk, and looked in.

Percy's tin box (nearly every boy in St. Maure's used a tin box for the keeping of let-ters, diaries, money, and small valuables) was open. The lock had been forced. There were iri it, besides a bundle of letters, some dozen and odd photographs. The letters were untouched; the photographs had been torn into halves— the photographs of Percy's mother and sisters.

"Poor Percy!" \'7bnought the prefect. "He'll feel this more than the loss of any sum of money. Could I only manage to keep him from knowing it! If I remember right, Percy had some money in this box. Yes, I'm sure of it. He spoke to me this morning about it. Peters has robbed him."

He shut the desk, and left the hall. "Charlie," he said to Richards, who was awaiting him outside, "you may suspect that Peters was in the study-hall for some other purpose. But be sure to say nothing about your meeting him here. Peters has run away. YouVe already guessed that, too ; but keep it a secret. You may tell the bovs at recess, if they ask about him, that he's

been expelled, which is a fact. Now, my boy, you may go back to your books."

After a short visit to the college president, the prefect^ on returning to his room, seated himself at his desk, and fell into a brown study.

Finally he seemed from his expression to have hit upon a solution of his difficulty; whereupon he took up his pen and wrote the following letter:

"DEAR MR. WYNN: I regret to say that Percy's photographs have been torn into halves. Percy's very sensitive, and—happily ignorant of his misfortune yet—I fear it would be a shock to him were he to learn that the pictures of those he loves so well have been thus rudely treated. The tearing, it seems, has been a bit of spite on the part of a boy who, I am ashamed to say, was, up to a few hours ago, a student of our college.

"I enclose you the mutilated photographs, and beg you to send me on at once their duplicates. Percy shall never know that these his most cherished reminders of his home-life have been thus desecrated.

"Yours sincerely in Ss. Cc.,

"FRANCIS MIDDLETON, S. J."

As he directed this letter, the bell for the five minutes' recess between study-hours sounded.

He hastened to the study-hall, and, as the last boy issued into the yard, took Percy's tin box, and brought it to his room.

When he came into the playground a moment later, he found that the wind, coming from north, was strong and biting. The boys, how* ever, who, under ordinary circumstances, were wont, when it changed to cold, to run and play with increased liveliness, were now for the most part gathered together in knots, and talking in low tones.

"Mr. Middleton," asked John Donnel, approaching in company with five or six of his companions, "is it true that Peters has been expelled ?"

"Yes, John. I hope it may be the last boy we shall lose this year." And Mr. Middleton, taking out his hand-bell, rang it as a signal for all to return to their books.

"Gracious!" added John. "It's getting awful ^old. I hope Peters doesn't stand on the platform to-night. Did he go by the six-forty-five train, sir?"

"Hurry up, or you'll catch cold, John," answered the prefect, hastening away.

But John's question haunted him for the hour ihat ensued. Did Peters take the six-forty-five train? It was an ugly night, and perhaps the wretched boy was out in it. If he had stolen a large sum of money, he would hardly dare to take the ordinary mode of traveling. Peters was old enough and shrewd enough to know that, were his robbery discovered that night, a telegram from the college would ensure detectives awaiting him at every depot from St. Maure's to Kansas City, where he lived.

In all probability, then, he had taken the road to Sykesville, a good two hours' walk. He had left the college about a quarter to seven. Hence,

in this event, he could hardly have more than made Sykesville by a quarter to nine.

Mr. Middleton drew out his watch: it was within five minutes of the hour.

u ln case he's walked, I hope he's at Sykesville," murmured the prefect, returning his watch to his pocket and hastening to the infirmary.

Our three friends were kneeling in prayer beside their beds, when, touching Percy lightly, he motioned him to come outside.

"Percy," he began, "how much money was in your tin box."

"Fifteen dollars, sir."

"I'm afraid, Percy, that youVe been robbed."

"Indeedy! Oh, I hope it's not a college boy that's the thief."

"I fear it is, though. Peters has run away, and it looks as though he stole the money."

"Poor fellow! Fm sorry for him. What a queer life he must have led!"

"Yes, Percy; but the money. What about that?"

"I don't mind the money, sir. Papa will send me more. But Fm sorry on account of that poor boy. He must be very unhappy."

"Well, Percy, please don't speak about this to anyone. We must try to save his reputation."

"That's so like you, Mr. Middleton. You're always thinking out how to save the feelings of other people. Fd never have thought of that, but I'd have gone and blurted out to every one that Peters was a thief. Thank you very much, Mr. Middleton; you've given me a new lesson in kindness."

If our little friend could have seen the letter addressed to his father, now on Mr. Middleton's desk, he would have appreciated still more the prefect's thoughtfulness.

"One thing more, Percy. I have taken your box to my room. Would you object to my keeping it for a few days? The lock has been broken, and things are upside-down. I'll return it to you in good condition. Have I your permission?"

"To keep it for a few days?" said Percy, effusively. "Mr. Middleto.n, you can keep it for a month—for a year— forever."

Smiling his thanks, the prefect bade Percy a hearty good-night. Percy received his box in due time, and, I believe, does not know to this day that the photographs, which he still cherishes, are not the photographs he brought to St. Maure's.

As the night advanced, it grew colder and colder. Mr. Middleton could not banish from his mind the thought of the runaway. The more he considered, the more he felt certain that Peters had not dared to take the train. Once his imagination got working upon this impression, the prefect began fancying all manner of dread possibilities. Would Peters even venture to seek a warm shelter? Peters, he remembered, was an adept at subterfuges. It would be of a piece with his character to keep clear of anything which might lead to his being traced.

The prefect retired at eleven of the night; but his imagination would not allow him rest. Hour after hour passed, and, wide-awake and

restless, he followed in fancy the steps of th$ wretched wayfarer.

At four o'clock, when the first gray gleaming of dawn moved along the eastern horizon, he arose, dressed, and, leaving the dormitory, took a turn in the garden fronting the main building.

"I can't stand it. I must go after that wretched boy—God help him 1 Shall I awake the president?" He glanced towards the president's room.

To his joy, he perceived a light shining from the windows.

Presently he was knocking at the door.

"Come in," said the president, rising from his knees. "Why, Mr. Middleton, what are you doing out of bed at this hour?"

"Father, I can't sleep. I've been thinking of Peters all night. Somehow, I can't get rid of the idea that he may be suffering from exposure. Would you kindly give me leave to go after him ? I'll be back in time for class."

The president had been scanning Mr. Mid-dleton's face closely.

"Yes," he made answer, "you may go—on one condition."

"Name it, Father."

"That on your return, you take the visitor's room and go to bed. I'll take your place in class, and I'll see that some one helps Mr. Kane in the yard. Of course, it's your duty to look after the boys; but it's mine to look after the teachers. You need a rest, my dear friend. Now, never mind, you needn't make any excuses. If you're not fast asleep by nine o'clock this morning, I'll send you off for a week's rest.

You've been worrying too much of late, and it's telling on you."

'Thank you, Father. Now please give me your blessing. I'm afraid I'll sleep but poorly if I don't find that boy."

Mr. Middleton fell upon his knees before him whom as a college boy he had known and loved.

With no little fervor, his superior blessed him, and, as he rose, added kindly, u God bless you."

And the eyes of the two met in a glance which rendered further words unnecessary.

A few minutes later Mr. Middleton was clattering along the frozen road to Sykesville. He reached the village before it was fairly light, and, to the no small disgust of many of the sleepy inhabitants, succeeded in learning that Peters had not set foot in the village.

By the time he had finished these inquiries, the dawn had grown to that sweet, soft, almost sacred light which is the immediate forerunner of sunrise. Mr. Middleton concluded that Peters was somewhere between the college and Sykesville; and accordingly he started back for St. Maure's slowly, carefully; not taking the road, but riding far and wide to right and left of the direct course, and examining every nook and recess which, in his judgment, Peters might have chosen for the night's shelter.

In this fashion, he had made about a mile and a half of his homeward journey, when he came upon three hay-stacks standing close together. He rode up to them, and, on turning to the farther side, saw Peters lying upon the earth, with his face to the ground.

Thanking God heartily, Mr. Middleton jumped from his horse, and caught the boy in his arms.

The sun was just then freeing its lower rim from the under-world, as Mr. Middleton, look* ing into the boy's face, gave a low cry of horror.

Peters was gagged. The fate he had designed for Tom and Harry he had met himself. Bound and gagged Peters had spent the night in the open air 1

In which are Set Down the Strange Advtn* tures of a Runaway

DETERS had just torn Percy's photographs, and was about to destroy his precious packet of letters, when the entrance of Richards brought his despicable bit of spite-work to a sudden end.

On leaving the study-hall the young thief found his way stealthily into the garden, and, sneaking along the walls of the infirmary building, crawled through a hole in the hedge-row bounding the college grounds to the northeast, and took the path along the railroad-track in the direction of Sykesville.

Mr. Middleton had conjectured aright. Peters had no thought of taking the train, no thought of even showing himself in the neighboring village. His plans were very simple. He would walk on till he had put six or seven miles between himself and the college, and would then seek some sheltered nook for the night. His manner of pressing on, by an odd coincidence, was not unlike Percy's on that very afternoon. He ran till his breath failed him; relaxed into a walk, and, when he had recovered his wind, broke into a run again.

Yes, their actions were singularly alike; but how different their motives 1

The young villain, however, had been guilty

125

of one oversight. He had forgotten to take his overcoat along. Heated as he was with running and rapid walking, he foresaw with dread and many a muttered curse that, unless he could find a very favorable shelter, it would go hard with him.

He had made another oversight— the oversight of his pitiful life. He had not brought with him the cloak of the soul, a good conscience. The gathering darkness, the lonely night, the wide-spread silence, broken only by the sobs and sighings of the northern blast, filled his soul with awful forebodings. There was a sinking at his heart, a presentiment of coming evil.

An hour and a half had passed, when he saw gleaming in the distance a few faint lights from the village. Well-nigh exhausted, the boy deserted the track, and, wandering about at haphazard, peered into the darkness in search of a favorable spot for his nights shelter.

Half an hour passed by in fruitless search, and he was about to abandon his quest in despair, when hope was aroused in him by the sight of a dark object looming up in his path.

He hastened forward, and gave a low cry of triumph upon discovering that he had come upon a row of hay-stacks. He forgot his fears, his forebodings, in the joy of his discovery. All would now be well. With a little trouble, he could burrow into one of the stacks, and crawling within, would be safe and warm for the night.

Without further ado, he began feeling about the b.ise of the nearest stack, in the hope of find-

ing a place already prepared. He had not proceeded far in his investigations, when, sure enough, he came upon an opening just such as he desired. He put in his hand, but withdrew it with a stifled cry.

"Cospetto!" came a voice. "Wat is dis?" And a rough head emerged from the hiding-place.

Waiting for no more, Peters took to his heels. But the gentleman he had disturbed was one of that class accustomed to decide promptly and act quickly. Peters had not cleared thirty yards, when a strong hand closing about his neck brought him to an abrupt stop.

He uttered a cry for help.

The hand on his neck tightened its grasp, till the boy's tongue protruded from his mouth.

"Bist I" hissed the strong Italian. 'You little bist, eef you make one oather ward, I weel choke you."

And turning the thoroughly frightened boy around, he conducted him to the hay-stack.

"Tim! Tim!" he whispered, "waken oop!"

"Shut your foreign mouth," came the answer from a rough looking, unshorn man of two or three and twenty. "I'm as wide-awake as ever I was. Who's that boy ?"

As the man spoke, he peered closely into Peters' face.

"I'm an orphan," chattered Peters, recovering from his fright sufficiently to lie. "I'm a poor boy with no home, and I'm looking for work. I felt so cold, I thought I might sleep here to-night. But if you'll please let me loose, I'll go on."

'Tim, what is de orphan? Does it sinyify a snick-a-teef ?"

This home-thrust, random arrow though it was, sent a shudder through the boy's frame.

"An orphan, you outlandish Garibaldian, is a feller as hasn't got no mother nor daddy."

The speaker was an Irish-American, the product of the large city, bad company, and a year or two of the public school. The man to whom he spoke would have been a "patriot" in our Italy of to-day, a "socialist" in a large American city; here and now, still true to the same spirit, he was an outlaw. The former came from the land of saints; the latter, from the land of art. American civilization has yet some riddles to read.

"Make not names ata me, Tim. Dees boy stole my money last summer. I remember me hisa face."

Here Peters struggled with what strength he had left to escape the inquisitorial hand of the young American. In return he received a strong open-handed blow on the face.

"You young devil," growled the fellow, "if you make another move, or speak above a whisper, I'll strangle you!"

He continued his search in the boy's pockets, while tears, due as much to vexation as to bodily suffering, coursed down the cheeks of his hapless victim.

"Ha! Fve got it! Bah! you little liar! 1 thought you had no money. Why, you're wealthy as a lord."

'Ow mooch?" inquired the Italian, his dark eyes gleaming.

"Thirteen — fourteen—fifteen dollars! Why, this is a windfall. Well, young feller, we'll let you take the hay-stack for the night. Our charges are moderate: I'll charge you seven-fifty for my share, and the yeller-face, there, will charge you the same for his share. You're in luck."

Peters sobbed and scowled in impotent rage.

"Nice-a little boy I" said the other. "We will now tie you oop, so you slip tight."

"Oh," cried Peters, finding words at prospect of this new calamity, "don't tie me! I won't tell; I give you my honor I won't tell. I'll get down on my knees and swear I won't tell."

"You can just bet you won't tell," said the native, forcing a handkerchief into the boy's mouth. "We'll not put you in under the hay, young feller," he continued, "or you'll never be found till you're starved to death. We'll leave you aut here. It's pretty cold; but we didn't make the weather. Some country-jake will find you to-morrow, I reckon; and then you can tell all you like. We'll be out of danger by that time. Good-night; hope you'll sleep well." And with this, the heartless villains left the lad to the bitter exposure, to the dark, and to his own thoughts.

To his own thoughts! Thoughts of a misspent life, memories of sin and evil deeds, prospects of death—exposed, alone, face to face with an invisible God Whose mercies had seemingly been drained. Fancy added to his fears. He could almost see the demons surging about him to take his soul to hell. The forlorn creature, suffering keenly from the cold, feared.

not without reason, that his death was imminent. What an awful coloring it gave his past life! Drops of sweat, the sweat of agony, froze upon his face, as sin after sin came back to his memory in all their horrid nakedness. As that foul procession passed in its unmasked, undisguised loathsomeness before his mind, he gradually began to entertain thoughts of despair. It was too late: his chances were past; hell now claimed him. In his heart, he was on the point of cursing himself, cursing God, when a sudden, gracious memory recurred to him.

Was it not but yesterday that Mr. Middleton, in catechism-class, had spoken so sweetly, so earnestly of God's infinite mercy? The whole Scene came back with a vividness which astonished the poor fellow.

Mr. Middleton had first said a few words about the necessity of contrition, then had put questions to the boys in order to ascertain whether they had taken his meaning.

"Harry Quip," he began, "answer me this. Suppose, my boy, that you had been a great sinner since you were capable of committing mortal sin; suppose that all your sins were still on your soul; that all your confessions had been bad, and you were suddenly to learn that you were to die here and now in this very room. Would you despair?"

"No, sir," answered Harry. "I would ask our blessed Mother to obtain grace for me to make an act of contrition, and then I would throw myself upon God's mercy."

"But suppose, Carmody," continued the pro*

fessor, "suppose that you had never done one single good act, and, on the other hand, suppose that you had upon your conscience all the sins that every boy now alive in the world had committed. What would you do in that case, were you to be told that you were to die at once?"

"I would confide in the infinite merits of the Precious Blood," answered Carmody.

'Joe Whyte, I will make the case stronger. With all these sins I have spoken of upon your soul, imagine yourself sinking, alone, compan-ionless, in mid-ocean; no priest near to absolve you, no kind friend to pray with you."

Joe answered with a certain elevation borrowed unconsciously from his teacher's words. "I would try with God's grace to make an act of perfect contrition, then I would sink into the sea as though I were sinking into the arms of God; for He is everywhere."

"A beautiful answer. But, Reynolds, suppose that God, in punishment of all these your sins, were to afflict you with a hideous disease. Suppose then that your friends were to fly from you in horror, that your relatives were to cast you out to live among beasts; suppose you were dying from exposure and want, and in the very moment of death you were to ask a priest to hear your confession, and that he, horrified by your loathsomeness, were to fly from you, crying out that God had already damned you. Would you yet despair?"

"No," Reynolds made reverent answer; "with God's grace, I would not even then despair."

"But I'll make the case more desperate, Daly. While thus loathsome you are dying, deserted by

the false priest, a crowd of demons come throng* ing about you, shrieking out that your soul is theirs, and that they have come to drag it away. Would you then despair?*'

The boy hesitated.

"I —I—think not," he answered at length.

s 'Quite right. But the case might be worse, Playfair. Suppose, in resisting these foul demons, that you called upon the angels of God and His saints, and they were all to answer you with one voice that it was too late. What then?"

"I wouldn't believe them, sir," answered Tom. "God's word is more to me than the words of the angels and saints."

"But suppose, Sommers, that our Blessed Lady herself were to assure you that it was too late."

"I—I'm afraid, sir, I'd give up."

"You would? Why?"

"Because Mary is too good a mother to deceive me."

"Not a bad reason. But could any one suggest a different answer?"

There was a long pause.

"I don't believe our Blessed Mother would
say such a thing, Mr. Middleton," said Tom.
'You've often told us she's the best friend of
sinners; and I'm sure she would be the last of
created beings to give a sinner up."

"But, for the sake of bringing out our point, let us suppose this impossible case, Tom. Would you despair?"

"No, sir; I wouldn't."

"Why not r

Tom had no answer. s-

"Do you think our Blessed Mother would de ceive you?"

Tom could neither affirm nor deny.

'Would you despair, Percy Wynn, if Mary were to tell you it was too late ?"

"No, sir. Her only possible meaning could be that it was too late in case I neglected to make an act of perfect contrition; because we know from God's holy Word that as long as we live we must not despair; and He has promised eternal life and His sweet grace to all who hope in Him and love Him."

"Boys, your answers are beautiful because they are so true. Let me add two quotations from that noble spiritual writer, Father Faber. 'At the day of judgment/ he says, 'I would rather be judged by God than by my own mother.' In another place he says, in speaking of dying sinners: 'God is infinitely merciful to every soul. . . . As to those who may be lost, I confidently believe that our Heavenly Father threw His arms about each created spirit, and looked it full in the face with bright eyes of love, in the darkness of its mortal life, and that of its own deliberate will it would not have Him.' Such, my dear boys, is the infinite and most tender mercy of God."

And then Peters remembered how Mr. Mid-dleton had covered his face and bowed his head, and how every boy in the room had lowered his eyes, and a silence like the peace of heaven settled upon all; while each, saving his own wretched self, stood face to face with the most

th'acious truth that God has made known to inan.

Then there came back to the sufferer, whose feet and arms were now numb with cold, the conversation he had held with Percy. Was there really an angel by his side —his own angel ? A great wave of divine love flooded the boy's soul, and for the first time in years he spoke to God in accents of true contrition; and even as he avowed his sorrow and his love, and gave thanks that God had thus rudely brought him to his senses, consciousness deserted him. *****

When he next opened his eyes, he found Mr. Middleton bending over him. They were in the sitting-room of a small country dwelling; beside the bed stood a doctor and the lady of the house.

"Thank God, Martin, that you're alive! Had I come upon you an hour later, the doctor says, it's doubtful whether you would ever have opened your eyes again."

Obeying a sign of the doctor's, the woman advanced and administered the boy a bowl of chicken-broth.

"Poor little fellow!" she murmured. "How beautiful he looked when the Father brought him in! I never saw a face so calm and peaceful.' 1

Mr. Middleton had himself been astonished at the change in Peters' features.

"The boy has been praying," was his comment. He had guessed the secret: the act of contrition which transformed the soul of Petera

at the moment of his sinking into unconsciousness had written itself upon his features.

But the lovely look left him with his coming to consciousness. To fix an expression such as he had worn upon the living face, years of high thought and holy purpose are necessary.

But though his face was unchanged, not so his spirit. The boy leaning upon Mr. Middleton's arm and gazing up so wonderingly into those kind eyes was not the boy of yesterday. The boy of yesterday was indeed dead.

"Little man," said the woman, "you're lucky to have such a friend as your teacher. If he hadn't taken off his own coats and wrappings, and half frozen himself to death on your account, and if he hadn't kept rubbing and chafing you, when he got here, till the doctor came, you'd not be alive to listen to me."

Peters caught his prefect's hand and kissed it reverently.

"I'm afraid Mrs. Burns is exaggerating, Martin."

"Indeed I'm not. I'm quite sure that if you've a pet among any of the boys, sir, that boy is the one, and no other."

"Mr. Middleton," whispered Peters, "can I see you alone?"

The doctor and Mrs. Burns withdrew, and in a long colloquy Peters told what was set down in the preceding chapter.

"To hear a story like that," said Mr. Middle-tons "is enough to make my memories of teaching grateful to the end of my days."

Then followed a conversation in which the prefect prepared Martin for some bitter trials^

Two of the poor boy's fingers, one on each hand, were to be amputated ; probably two. He would be a cripple for life.

"I am willing to suffer," answered Martin, undismayed. "I have been a bad boy; I hope God will take my sufferings in payment."

"Martin, I have to tell you another unpleasant thing. You— you're not to come back to college."

"I wouldn't think of it, Mr. Middleton. It would be wrong for you to keep a known thief among the boys."

"Not known," came the answer. "Percy Wynn is the only one in the college who knows you have taken his money, and, you may be sure, he'll never speak of it. I can go even farther: Percy will forgive you the debt, and every one of our class will remember you kindly, and pray for you, when, as you have requested me, I tell them your adventures of last night, leaving out, of course, all mention of the stolen money."

"Mr. Middleton, I have not deserved this from you."

"Ah! there's another thing, Martin: be very careful, when you write to Percy, not to mention the fact of your having torn his photographs. I trust that Percy will never find that out. You and I are the only two who, as yet, know anything about that matter. Here are five dollars, my poor boy; by this evening you will be able to take the train for home. I shall telegraph your father to meet you at the depot. Now I must go. It's eight o'clock, and I'm un>

der orders to be asleep by nine. Good-by, my friend."

Mr. Middleton held out his hand.

The boy caught it and covered it with kisses.

"Oh, I can't say it!" he sobbed. "I can't—I can't— God help me 1"

Mr. Middleton was moved. 'We shall meet again," he said softly; "and I shall remember you daily in my prayers, and, if you wish, I'll write to you."

'Thank you! thank you!" said Peters, in tones which gave the words full meaning. 'Well, good-by," said the prefect.

But Peters turned his face to the wall and sobbed as though his heart were breaking.

CHAPTER XIV

In which Percy Finds Himself on the Sick-list

Percy awoke next morning, the SUP was up and shining brightly through thp infirmary windows. He made an attempt tc arise, but discovered to his astonishment that hf was scarcely able to turn in his bed.

Tranquilly resigning himself to the situation, he made the sign of the cross and recited his morning prayers; which he had scarcely concluded, when the Brother entered bearing on a tray tea and toast, eggs and beefsteak.

'What a lazy boy you are!" he said. "At your age you should rise with the lark. Jump up ! put on your clothes, and take a run about the grounds and get an appetite for breakfast." 'The spirit is willing," said Percy, with a smile, "but the flesh is weak. And besides, I don't think my appetite needs so much care at present."

The Brother bolstered him into a sitting position, and set the tray beside him on a small table.

"Now help yourself."

"Brother, I want to ask you a question. Don't you think it looks queer for a boy of my age and size to go around with his hair hanging down to his shoulders?"

"It's very pretty, perhaps," answered the in-

firmarian, cheerfully, "but it is certainly uncommon here."

"That's just what I've been thinking," said Percy, reflectively. "And besides, it isn't convenient for a boy, though I suppose it may be all right for girls. It gets in the way so often, you know. Sometimes when I am playing catch, my hair comes tumbling over my eyes, and that makes me muff worse than I would do otherwise. Indeed, if I didn't have hair at all, I don't think I'd hold one ball in twenty—I have such butter-fingers, as Tom says. Yes; I think I'll have it cut short. I don't want people to think I'm proud."

"Very good," said the Brother, who had listened to these naive confessions with ill-suppressed amusement. "When you're limber enough to leave the infirmary, I'll cut your hair myself."

Percy contrived to make a fair breakfast, and had hardly finished, when who should enter but Charlie Richards!

"Why, how do you do, sir?" said Percy in some astonishment. "Won't you take a seat? Do. Bring a chair over here by my bed: I regret that I am unable to rise."

The invalid was quite serious as, with the grand air of a young prince, he made his polite requests, tendered his apologies.

Richards, somewhat confused by this anomalous reception, brought a chair beside Percy, and seated himself.

"Percy, I've come to ask your pardon," he began. "I'm awfully ashamed of myself, and I'm very glad you spoiled our mean plot. Would you mind shaking hands?"

"Certainly not," answered Percy, warmly. "I'm very glad you and I have come to be friends; and I guess it's mostly my fault that you haven't liked me. I'm so stuck-up, you know. I came here like a young peacock, and strutted around as if I weren't a boy at all. I'm not one bit surprised now that the boys teased me, and pulled my hair sometimes, and threw it over my eyes when I was trying to catch a ball. I'm sure they wanted to teach me; for they were nearly always so good-natured. Indeed, my only surprise is that they didn't plague
me more."

Percy was entirely serious. Like the noble-hearted child he was, he had a habit of looking upon everything from the bright side ; and even those of the very thoughtless or cruel boys who had shown him unkindness he had come to look upon as his benefactors.

"Aren't you making fun of me?" asked Richards.

"No, indeed! But I hope you're not going to be punished."

"No; but I ought to be. Mr. Middleton has begged me off. The very first thing this morning, Tom Playfair came to me and asked me to shake hands."

"Oh, it's so like Tom!" said Percy with enthusiasm. "He's the best boy I ever met. If Pancratius were alive to-day, he'd be something like Tom; I know he would."

"Indeed he is a splendid fellow," said Richards, earnestly. "And I wish I had got to know
him when I first came here, instead of falling in with Peters. You know he's been expelled, don't you?"

"I heard of it last night," said Percy.

Richards, who was a fluent talker, related graphically the last night's scene in the study-hall.

u Poor fellow!'* said Percy, sadly. "We must pray for him. How his mamma must feel about it!"

"He has no mother, he told me once: she died when he was little more than a baby."

"Oh dear, dear! No wonder he wasn't a very good boy. I'm sure if it hadn't been for my mamma and my sisters to care for me, I'd have been a villain. I know I would. It almost makes me cry, sometimes, when I think of poor boys growing up without a mother's love, and with no one to take the mother's place. They have such poor chances."

"It is indeed hard," assented Richards.

"And then to think of those boys not of our faith who have no mother here and no Mother Mary in heaven—no Blessed Virgin to help them, no mother at all."

"I'm going to try to join the sodality," said Richards. "I haven't been what I ought to be, so far. In fact, I haven't used a pair of beads for over a year."

"Oh gracious!" exclaimed Percy. "No wonder you fell into bad company."

"Well, I've learned a few things the last few days," Richards resumed, "and I'm going to make a new start."

"Do," said Percy, earnestly, "and I'm sure we'll be good friends."

Contrary to prevailing custom, there were no games going on in the yard after breakfast. The students were grouped into two crowds, one about Harry Quip, the other about Tom, each of whom was holding forth with eloquence on Percy's great achievement.

"I used to think he wasn't much of a boy," said Tom, "but now I don't think I'm half as much of a boy as he is."

Greatly to Tom's delight, the prefect of studies, summoning him before studies, informed him that he might absent himself from Latin and Greek schools for the present (Tom was leader in both these branches), and give the time to teaching Percy.

Percy was, if possible, even more pleased. Sitting up in bed, when his young professor had inaugurated class, he rattled off the five declensions, the adjectives of three, two and one endings, the personal, possessive, and demonstrative pronouns—everything, in fact, as far as the verb.

"You know it like a book," said Professor Tom, "and I must say that I am —ahem !—more than — ahem !—gratified. Now let's apply your knowledge. We'll begin with something easy. What's the Latin for rose ?"

"E>^o/i "

l\OSCl.

"Exactly, genitive ros<z, of the first declension, and feminine, because words of the first declension have a way of being always feminine. And for moon?"

"Luna."

"Quite correct," said the professor, gravely. "And from luna comes lunatic and lunacy, which is a learned way of saying moonstruck. Now say this, and be careful about it, or you'll choke: To the roses of the moon."

"To-the-roj^-of-the-/////^/' said Percy, innocently.

The professor began laughing, and turned away his head to recover himself: he considered it unprofessional to laugh in the face of his pupil.

"Not correct, Percy. Look here: are there any articles in the Latin language ?"

"Oh, that's a fact," said Percy. "Now I've got it, sure. To rosa of luna. There, now."

"That's a little better. But what is 'to' a sign of?"

"Of the dative case."

"Just so. Now we're getting there. And then what is 'of a sign of?"

"The genitive."

"Precisely. And in Latin, instead of using 'to' or 'of,' which are not Latin words at all, but common English, we simply put the word in the proper case."

"Oh, what a goose I was !" said Percy. "Now I understand the whole matter— Rosis luna"

"You're there now. Now say: To the rose of the moons."

"Rosa lunar um."

Tom twisted these words in all possible ways, then threw in an adjective, then a verb; and having an uncommonly bright pupil to deal with, he succeeded, within the short space of one hour,

in initiating Percy into the mystery of Latin cases and agreement.

"You're a good pupil, Percy. For your next lesson take the indicative mood of the verb esse, *to be.' '

"Very good. But, Tom, I don't like the way of changing the nouns in Latin for every case. In English it's much simpler. We keep the noun the same, but make the difference by using 4 to' or 'for' or 'with,' or some such little word."

"I don't know that it's so much easier," answered Tom. "Did you ever hear a boy of foreign birth struggling with English prepositions and expressions?"

"No. Do they find it hard?"

"I should say so. The other day John Boes, a German boy in our class, who boards in St. Maure's village, told our teacher that he had lost his written theme under the way to school."

"Oh, what a funny expression!"

"Isn't it? And he told me, once I got talking with him, that he lived by his uncle's house, and that he took dinner by his grandmother every day out of the week."

"Oh my!"

"And in one of his class-compositions describing Spring, he wrote : 'The little chickens run around rapidly, and stuff themselves full of green grass/

Percy laughed so that he shook every nerve and muscle, and was minded by his soreness to restrain himself.

"And in another of his compositions, which 1 shall never forget," continued Tom, "he de^ scribed the way he spent one of his holidays.

It was short but interesting, so I learnt it by heart. It ran this way: 'I stood up from my bed at a quarter behind six, and I washed my eyes out and my neck off, and combed down my hair. I spent the rest of the day by my grandmother in the country, who wears green spectacles.'

Percy could hardly restrain himself from violent laughter. His sense of humor was keen, and Tom's imitative powers were fairly good.

But all fun aside, Tom was correct in his opinion. Boys of foreign birth, in learning English have great difficulty in handling prepositions and connecting words. The Latin tongue, with its clearly defined cases and set rules of grammar, they find to be far more easy.

In the afternoon the private lessons were resumed; and Percy's progress was most encouraging to the learned professor.

"If you stay here another week," said Tom, "you'll know more Latin than I."

Next day Percy received a visit from Mr* Middleton.

"How's the young tramp?" he inquired.

"Oh, I'm just splendid!" answered Percy. "Everybody's so nice and kind. And see what a fine easy-chair I'm in. I can notice my improvement every hour, almost. To-day I found I could walk a little; and in a few days or so my legs will be as good, or rather as bad as ever."

"Don't you find it lonesome here?"

"Oh dear! no. Tom and I have grand Latin classes. He's given me four lessons already, of an hour each, and I'm now nearly through the verb amo, and have already begun translating the Historic Sacra. I've made out the first six chapters by myself. Then, you know, when I get tired of studying, I've got 'Dion and the Sibyls/ It reminds me of 'Ben Hur.' Both of them are splendid books."

"It's a great gift to like good reading," said the prefect. "Whether sick or well, we can always read. For myself, I must say that books have lent happiness to many of my spare hours."

"That's so," said Percy, who, it should be remembered, previous to coming to St. Maure's had associated almost entirely with persons older than himself. "A really good book brings us into good company. When I've been reading about noble and brave men, I feel just as if I had been spending my time with them."

"Yes ; but the pity is that the reverse is equally true. Those boys who are constantly reading about low characters and vile conduct come from their books as if they had been in evil company. These cheap detective and Indian stories— many of them, at least —do more harm than people in general imagine. I wish all boys were of your way of thinking, Percy. Some won't read anything unless they know that there are Indians to be kille' 4 , or trains to be robbed, or mysterious and blood-curdling murders to be explained."

"Mamma says that people Jike such stories only because they've been trained badly. She says that all boys are naturally good and religious, and naturally love what is brave and beau-' tiful and noble; but by being led to consider fighting as brave, and slang as witty, they look

upon everything the wrong way—'from the seamy side,' she used to say."

'Your mamma is right. I wish all the mammas in the land had her ideas."

"Oh, Mr. Middleton, she's coming here during the Christmas holidays. I want to introduce you. I know she'll like you ever so much."

"Indeed!"

"Oh yes, indeed. I like you, Mr. Middle-ton,"— Percy, be it remembered, was by no means bold or forward. It was in beautiful simplicity he thus spoke to the prefect, just as he was wont to speak to mother and sisters,— "and I want you to know all my sisters. They are nice girls: but they weren't one bit kinder to me at home than you've been here."

"Well, good-by," said the prefect, laughing. "I'm bashful and not used to being complimented, so I'd better retire. When you feel very grateful to me again, please pay your gratitude out in prayer for me."

"Oh, indeed I will. I do pray for you every day, Mr. Middleton, and I intend keeping it up. And I'll get my sisters to join in, too. They're far better at it than I am."

"Well, good-by."

And the prefect departed wondering.

CHAPTER XV

"From Grave to Gay" — A Serious Converse tion, Followed by a Game of Foot-ball

TT WAS the afternoon of the eighth day since

Percy's entrance Into the infirmary. He was now in good health, but, as a matter of prudence, was still kept on the sick-list.

Tom entered to give his last private lesson in Latin. He found Percy reading a letter from home.

"You're just in time, Tom; here's a message for you. It's from sister Mary. She says: 'Tell your magnificent little friend Tom Playfair that we are all full of gratitude to him for the kindness and painstaking he has bestowed on our dear little brother. If prayers and good wishes may help him on, they shall never be wanting.' And here's something else, Tom."

He handed Tom a lace picture of the Blessed Virgin.

"It's from Minnie."

"Minnie?"

'Yes: she's my youngest sister, only six years old. She wants sister Mary to let me know that she likes Tom Playfair better than all her sisters, except, perhaps, sister Mary. (She has her doubts even about this exception.) And she wants it known to the whole family that if she's riot allowed a more liberal allowance of cake and candy, she'll run off and tell Tom Playfair on them. Oh, she's so funny, Tom ! Sometimes she makes a regular speech. She can talk wonderfully well for a child of six."

'What must the rest of them be," thought Tom, "if the baby-girl can make speeches! If ever any of them come this way, I think I'll run away myself."

"Tom," continued Percy. "I've another very beautiful letter."

'Which sister?" asked Tom with a grin.

"From Martin Peters. He says he would have written me before, only he couldn't use his hand. He will have to stay in bed all winter; but the doctor assures him that he will be able to use his feet again just the same as though they had never been frost-bitten."

"That's good news," said Tom. "But the poor fellow will have to go minus two fingers for the rest of his days. What more does he say?"

"He begs my forgiveness, and asks my prayers, and writes me all manner of nice things."

"Peters is in earnest," said Tom. "He wrote me a letter, too; I got it by this morning's mail. He said so many nice things to me in it that I blushed and tore it up."

"Did you?"

"Just so. He's studying privately, and is going in early spring to an Eastern Catholic college. I guess there was a special providence in his having been exposed that awful night."

"God was 'cruel only to be kind,' ' assented Percy.

"I wonder," thought Tom, "where Percy raked up that quotation?"

"I say, Percy," he continued aloud, "there's one thing about you which has puzzled me a good deal."

"Indeed! you surprise me. I have never seen you look much astonished of late at anything I said or did. I thought you had got used to me."

"So I have, in a way. But there's one thing I can't explain. Most boys coming from home to boarding-school for the first time get dreadfully homesick, and lose their cheerfulness. Now I haven't noticed any change in you at all."

"Well, it is funny, I thought I would be. But I believe I can explain it. It's this way. In the first place, I fell in with good boys, and kind ones too, at once. They've treated me so nicely that sometimes I'm positively ashamed of myself ; for I know I don't deserve it at all. Then besides, there's the novelty of fishing, swimming, base-ball, and all sorts of games. It's like a new world to me."

"Yes, that's all right for the first month or so," said Tom. "But what about this last week in the infirmary? You haven't had the novelty of out-door games, and, besides, you were often alone. I was sure you'd get homesick in here."

Percy paused before answering.

'Well, Tom, I don't mind telling you; but I've got a friend I always try to keep by me. And when I feel inclined to be sad, I do what my mother advised me to do when we bade each other good-by—I talk to it. See?"

He drew from his pocket a morocco case,

opened it, and disclosed to Tom's eyes a beauti* ful picture of the Sacred Heart.

Tom's face expressed genuine pleasure.

"That's a capital idea!" he said.

"Indeed it is," assented Percy. "Sister Mary gave me it. And really I find by experience that a few words with the Heart of Jesus do give me strength."

"I've got a plan something like that myself," said Tom, as he drew a rather worn scapular of the Sacred Heart from his pocket. "John Don-nel gave me the idea. It's not much to look at, I know. But when I feel like getting angry or sulky, or grow tired studying, or anything goes wrong, I just put my hand in my pocket, and catch hold of it. That brings me to time regularly."

One week later, if we may anticipate, Torn received a small parcel by the mail. It contained a morocco case enclosing a picture, both identical with Percy's. On a slip of paper accompanying the gift were the words: "With the compliments of Mary Wynn."

"I'm glad to learn that you know something about the devotion to the Sacred Heart," continued Tom; "for I intended speaking to you on this very point. Some of us boys have a little association in private. Keenan is at the head of it, and Donnel, Quip, Whyte, Ruthers, Granger, and eight or nine more are members. We all observe certain easy rules, and it seems to do a great deal of good. The president of the college knows of it, and likes it very much."

"You don't say!" exclaimed Percy. "That's just splendid! No wonder so many of the boys here are so good, and so kind, too, to queer people like me. Of course I'll be delighted to join it."

Tom explained the rules in a few words.

The writer has at his hand the whole scheme of this little association, with the names of all the members up to a certain year. But as the association may, for aught he knows, be still in existence he thinks it prudent not to infringe on their privacy by divulging their simple rules.

"And now for our lesson," pursued Tom. 'We've seen nearly everything in Latin as far as the class has gone, except a few rules in syntax and ninety-five lines of Firl Roma. I really think you can afford to take a rest this afternoon. Even with ordinary study I'm sure you'll be up with the class in a few weeks."

'Very good. I like Latin immensely, Tom, since you've given me a good start; and now I'm really glad I had to take this week in the infirmary. I've been able to give all my time to Latin, and I'm well enough up in all other branches of our class."

"It's about time to come out into the fresh air, though," said Tom. "I want to show you something about foot-ball. It's been cool weather ever since the night you came in, and it's too chilly for base-ball any longer."

Next morning, Percy, with his hair close-cropped^ made his appearance in the yard. He was received with almost an ovation. The students crowded around him, eagerly pressing forward to shake his hand. What with the honors thus showered upon him, and what with the feeling that he must look "so queer" with his

golden hair cut short, Percy blushed so violently and became so confused, that honest John Don-nel, with a fine delicacy, forced his way through the crowd, caught him up, and carried him off.

"Come on, boys," he cried, "we're going to play foot-ball, and Percy's on my side."

There were at each end of the yard two posts seven feet high, joined together at the top by a cross-bar seven feet in length. These were the "goals" of the respective sides: and it was the object of each of the contending forces to keep the ball from entering his own goal, and to kick it, if possible, into that of his opponents. The foot-ball was to be touched only with the feet, with one exception. This was when a ball kicked in the air could be secured before it touched the ground. In this case it could be "punted" — struck with the fist—or again the catcher had the privilege of running with it, if he could. But even then, in delivering it, Jhe was obliged to put it on the ground and kick it from that position. Kicked from his hands it would be a "foul," and should it reach the goal, the play would not count.

These rules, with others less important, were quickly explained to Percy, and he was assigned a station midway between the two goals.

"You see," said Tom, conducting him to his position, "the chances are, you'll miss the ball every time you try to kick it ; but it doesn't matter so much, far off from the goal. If we were to put you up closer to Keenan's goal, it wouldn't matter so much either, only you'd run the risk of getting shinned in a crowd."

"But wouldn't it be better, for the first time, if I were to play near our own goal?"

"Not by any manner of means. If you were to miss a kick there, you might lose the game on us. Now you know where you're to stand, come back behind this line till the ball is kicked off. Now keep your eyes open: Donnel's going to take first kick."

The ball was placed about fifty feet in front of John's goal. Each side put itself in position: Donnel's side (which, for convenience, we will call our side) a little behind the ball, and Kee* nan's back of a fixed line fronting their goal.

"Ready?" cried Donnel.

"Kick away!" answered the captain of the opposing side.

Moving back a few feet, Donnel ran forward, and with a vigorous kick sent the ball spinning into the air.

The scene of life and animation which immediately ensued beggars description. Percy was utterly amazed. Just a moment before, he had been standing in a crowd of some forty or fifty boys, all perfectly quiet, facing an equally large crowd which, save for their bright, eager eyes, seemed to be without life or motion. Now all was changed. As the Rugby ball rose in the air, a rousing cheer broke from a hundred lusty throats, then a quick patter and stamping of feet, and a hundred lads jostling, crowding, hastening forward in pursuit of the ball.

"Come on, Percy!" cried Tom, putting a period to the novice's contemplation. "Don't stand there star-gazing : look alive!"

Catching him by the arm, Tom rather unceremoniously hurried him forward to his place.

All this was enacting while the ball was still in the air. It was going straight towards our opponent's goal. But one of the goal-keepers, Kennedy, a tall, thin youth, made a spring into the air, and caught it on the fly.

"Run it! run it!" shouted his side.

"Drop it! drop it!" yelled our fellows, who were making for Kennedy with a speed which promised to settle the question out of hand.

Kennedy was evidently unused to the game. He hesitated. Now, in foot-ball, the boy who hesitates is lost. He slowly made up his mind to "run it," but before he had barely taken one step forward, Donnel was upon him, and with a clever rap sent the Rugby flying out of his hands.

But it was another thing to kick the ball in, lying though it was just in front of Keenan's goal. As it fell to the ground, our side came up in great numbers, and, cheered on by their leader and his lieutenants, made vigorous efforts to clear the ball through the opposing ranks.

"Stand by the goal!" roared the enemy. And they did stand by it to the full of their skill.

In the meantime, Percy wondered ^what had become of the ball. There was no sight of it. Nothing to be seen but a compact mass of boys kicking, pushing, panting, shouting—all earnest, none angry.

Tom, stationed a few yards^to Percy's right, was amusing himself by practising hand-springs.

Percy interrupted his exercise with the question: "Where's the ball, Tom?"

"That's what everybody's trying to find out," said Tom.

"Goodness me!" continued Percy, shaking back his hair in imagination—such is the force of habit —"I never thought that so large a crowd of boys could pack themselves up so tightly. How many are there, Tom?"

"Everybody except you, me, Johnson there, and our six goal-keepers. About ninety in all. Keep your eyes open, Percy; the ball may come flying your way any moment."

But the jam and push still continued.

"Crowd it out ! crowd it out 1" rang the battle-cry of our opponents.

"Force it in! force it in!" answered our side.-

"Playfair," shouted Donnel above the din, "come on and help us. Bring up all the goal-keepers except two; we must crowd it in."

"Stay here, Percy," said Tom. He added in a much louder voice : "All of you goal-keepers, come up on a run except Ruthers and Sommers."

But before these words of command were well free of Tom's mouth, the ball came with a bound out of the crowd, amid wild applause from the enemy. As the fates had arranged matters, it was coming through the air straight towards Percy, who stood looking at it in wonder and awe.

Our side was filled with dismay.

"Run back to the goal—quick!" yelled Don-fiel.

Suddenly another cheer arose, drowning out the triumphant clamoring of the enemy. Tom Playfair, anticipating Percy's inability to act, had on a dead run captured the ball within a

foot of the ground, and was now dashing on towards Keenan's goal.

So quickly had all this come to pass that the boys who had been innermost in the pack had scarce fully disengaged themselves. Hence only a few of the enemy were in Tom's vicinity.

"Head him off! Stop him! Take the ball from him!" cried those of the enemy nearest the goal, as they pressed forward.

But not only was Tom a speedy runner; he was an expert, too, in the art of dodging. Already by his adroitness had he given three of the enemy the slip, and in successfully avoiding a fourth, he ran with full force into a fifth (unintentionally, of course), and sent him sprawling. He was now within fifty feet of the goal, and had no time to lose, for the enemy were upon him close. Flashing the ball to the ground, he gave it a straight kick. It made directly towards the goal. There was a dismal groan from the enemy, followed in almost the same breath by their shout of joy. The ball had overshot the goal-posts.

Keenan ran back and secured the ball, which was now "out of bounds." According to the rules of the game as played at St. Maure's he was now entitled to bring the ball forward to an imaginary straight line from the goal, and to give it a "free kick," i. e., without being molested by our men, who could not touch it till it had left his hands.

Once in motion, the scuffling and pushing began afresh; but this time the ball was not lost under hurrying feet. Indeed it was not suffered to touch the ground at all. Beaten from hand

to hand, or rather from fist to fist, it seemed to play like a dimmed glory above the players' heads. One boy with a vigorous blow would send it towards the enemy's goal, and another, jumping into the air and reaching it with his hand, would drive it back. So, for some minutes, the ball seemed to fly from hand to hand, like a butterfly in a garden of flowers. Suddenly it touched ground, and before one could so much as take a breath, a quick kick from Keenan sent it high over the heads of the punters straight towards Percy. To the surprise of everyone, especially to his own, Percy caught it.

"Hurrah!" shouted Tom. "Run, Percy, and kick it as soon as any of the other fellows get near you."

Percy's eyes shone with excitement. He looked towards Keenan's goal, and saw the whole path blocked with breathless, hurrying boys. But towards our goal he perceived all was clear.

"Hurrah!" he shouted, and turning, he set off with all speed towards his own goal.

"Hold on, Percy! Come back! the other way!" bawled Tom. But his words were drowned in the general noise, and Percy in his innocent but misdirected zeal sped on. No one being prepared for this strange proceeding, he was actually within a few feet of our goal before his progress was arrested, having, to the general astonishment, successfully evaded two of his own men, Johnson and Sommers.

But when he came face to face with Harry Quip, he stopped of his own free will.

"Here, Harry, 1 ' he said, "what shall I do with it?"

"Give it to me, quick!" said Harry; and taking the ball, he put it to the ground hurriedly, and sent it whirling on high back to the middle of the yard.

"What did you do that for?" Percy inquired in great surprise.

"Look here, Percy," answered Harry, "the object of this game isn't to kick the ball anywhere, or run anywhere with it; nor is it to kick it towards any goal, or run it towards any goal. The idea is to get it through the goal of the other side. Just now you were playing against us; and you ran so well with those stiff old legs of yours that you nearly lost us the game."

"You don't say!" Percy exclaimed. "Oh, I'm so sorry! You must excuse me this time, Harry. Next chance I get, you'll see I'll play right." And Percy, with his ideas more coherently arranged on the subject of foot-ball, resumed his position in the field.

He had scarcely taken his place, when another psean of excitement rang through the startled air.

"Head him off!" "Pull him down!" "Stop him!" "Hold him!" "Catch him!" "Keenan's got the ball!" "Hurrah for Keenan!"

Such were the excited voices that broke from the throng, as Keenan, with the ball locked in his arms, forced his way, panting and breathless, towards our goal.

Keenan was rather undersized for his years; but he was of muscle all compact, and could run like a deer. With the force of a young

battering-ram, he shot by several of our side. A few of our boys made weak attempts to arrest his course, but it was plain that they had but little heart to beard him directly. He was now nearing Tom's station, and that young player, who was not easily frightened, made a bold dash at him. George took a quick turn to one side; but his adversary was no less quick, and caught George's arm, to which he held on grimly. But George was of uncommon strength, and redoubling his efforts, he went right on, dragging, almost carrying, his assailant. The excitement, now at its high-water mark, became so contagious that even Percy for the nonce became a spirited foot-ball player. In his turn he made a bold dash at Keenan, but, missing him, he chanced to catch Tom.

The added weight was too much for Keenan. He lost his balance, and fell back, the ball rolling to one side. Tom was up in an instant. He gave the ball a slight but well-aimed kick, sending it straight to Donnel, who, stopping it with his hand, placed it in position and, before the enemy could guard home, sent it flying through their goal. The game was ours.

Percy, then, without so much as kicking the ball — it was several weeks later before he acquired the knack —had been an important factor in the victory.

In which Mr. Middleton Reads a Story, and Excites Much Interest

TT WAS now early in December. Time, who treats us as we treat him, had flown swiftly and pleasantly for our little friends. An unbroken round of play and study had developed both mind and body. For many, many days not a single serious unpleasantness had marred the general good-feeling. With the departure of Peters, a local golden age seemed vo have dawned. Richards had become one of the foremost boys in good. He had given up his former friends, and was now constantly in the company of the best and most promising students. And to our young friends in particular, with whom he had become intimate, he proved to be an acquisition. It soon appeared that he was a boy of much general information. For his age he had read much. But this, in fact, had been at the root of many of his faults. He had not been carefully watched over at home; and, following his bent, had given much of his time to reading cheap, sensational, juvenile stories, which, without being always ill-intended or positively bad, hold up to their readers false ideals of beauty and of heroism. There are many earnest and generous-natured boys who, without even perceiving it, are led astray through such writings. The harm is rarely done with the

161

perusal of a single volume, or even of a second or a third: it is the joint result of many.

One day Richards brought Mr. Middleton a cheap, paper-covered book, asking him whether he considered it fit reading.

U I never saw any harm in it myself, sir," said Richards, frankly. "But since late events, I've come to think that my judgment isn't so good on such subjects."

"Thank you, Richards," said Mr. Middleton. "I am glad to see that you are in so earnest a temper. You are probably right in doubting. I think, on the face of it, that this book is far more dangerous than you can imagine at present. However, I shall examine it more carefully, and give you an honest criticism."

The book was an account of a boy's adventures at a school and elsewhere. It was written in a crisp, clipped style, and represented the hero as a lad of sixteen, who feared nothing, who was witty, inventive, full of animal spirits, and, in short, possessed apparently of every quality capable of awakening the enthusiasm of young readers.

It failed, however, to awaken Mr. Middle-ton's sympathy, and on the following day, towards the end of class, he said: "I am going to read you a little story."

There was a buzz of enthusiasm, and a great shifting of positions. It is impossible for the average boy, while in the class-room, to hear the announcement of a story with equanimity. Every one brightens up, and adjusts himself to what he considers to be the most receptive attitude. Those in the back seats are quite wretched

unless allowed to move towards the front; while those in front wish to get yet nearer to the teacher's desk. All crowd together, as far as the professor will admit, and glance sternly at any luckless youth who may chance to cough or make the least undue noise. There is a wondrous fascination for youngsters in a story. All boys are idealists.

"Conticuere omnes, intentique ora tenebant" And Mr. Middleton began his reading. It was a chapter from the book which Richards had given him. The school which the hero attended was to have its yearly picnic. One of the professors, who spoke broken English and was the butt of all the scholars, had signified his intention of attending on horseback, but possessing no equestrian skill, was very anxious to obtain a suitable steed. Here the funny hero came to the rescue. He persuaded the professor that he knew just what kind of a horse would suit him; then went to a livery stable and hired the most villainous nag in the establishment. Of course a great many ludicrous adventures follow; and the professor simply succeeds in escaping with life and limb. As Mr. Middleton reads of the professor's predicament, all the boys seem amused, while many laugh heartily. Percy, the only exception, appears to be pained.

"So you laugh, do you?" said the teacher, throwing down the book. "Well, what are you laughing at?"

The smiles vanished under Mr. Middleton's serious glance. Everybody began to wonder whether there had not been some mistake in their approbation.

"I ask again, why did you laugh? There must be some reason. You don't laugh when a sum in fractions is explained. You don't laugh at the Latin verbs. Why did you laugh just now?"

"I think," said Harry Quip, who was seldom puzzled for an answer, "we laughed because the story is written so funnily. n

"That's good," said the prefect. "I am glad that you have a reason. So, then, it seems the story is funnily told. But now I ask, is the story itself really funny?"

The class knit its brows. This was a hard question.

Suddenly Percy's hand went up.

"Well, Percy."

"It seems to me, Mr. Middleton, that the story itself is really not funny, but is made to appear so by the author's manner of treating

it."

'That's a very good answer indeed. You are quite right. The story itself is very sad. And now, boys, let me tell you what you have been laughing at; you have been laughing at the rowdyish actions of a rowdy."

The boys gazed at each other in a dazed fashion.

"But don't think I am angry or disappointed with you," pursued Mr. Middleton. "You are too young as yet to perceive the underside of such things at once. Just as a skilled counterfeiter can palm off his false money on many ordinary grown people, and on very intelligent children, so a writer may cause boys to accept

as really good what is, in point of fact, utterly vile."

Richards, who had given every word his utmost attention, here raised his hand.

"Well, Charlie?"

"Please, Mr. Middleton, show us how that story is bad. I began to see in a dim sort of way that what you say is true, but nothing is very clear to me."

"Very good. Now let us consider what the substance of the story is. Here we have, to begin with, an awkward man, but still a teacher, and consequently entitled to the respect of the students. He wishes to ride to a picnic. The hero, knowing that the teacher is no horseman, promises to procure him a gentle horse. He promises in all seeming sincerity. He lies. The story, then, is founded on a lie. What does the hero actually do? He hires a veritable spit-fire. Now, will some one please answer me this question? Suppose a man utterly ignorant of even the rudiments of horsemanship undertakes to mount a dangerous animal under the impression that it is quiet and tame, what will happen? What do you say, Sommers?"

"The chances are that he'll be killed."

"And you, Percy?"

"Oh dear! I can't bear to think of it."

"And you, Playfair?"

"Well, if he weren't killed, at least there'd be a good many chances to nothing that he'd be hurt—get his leg or his arm broken, any. how."

"Just so. He might be killed— that is possi-

ble. But it would certainly be extraordinary if he were to come off unhurt. In planning a trick, we have no right to trust our victim's escaping serious evil through extraordinary chances. Now this jolly hero, who, according to the story, is wise enough to be responsible for his actions, — and old enough too, being sixteen, — deliberately, or at least recklessly, and for the sake of a laugh, imperils the limbs, if not the life, of a human being, of one who is over him and certainly entitled to his respect."

The boys looked at each other: how the face of the story had already changed!

"This brings me back to the lie," resumed Mr. Middleton after a short pause. "It was a lie told concerning a very serious matter. It was a lie the telling of which might result, in its after-effects, in a broken arm or leg, in long sickness, or even in death. Such a lie is indicative of gross thoughtlessness; it is unworthy of any story-book hero,

"And further, what is the result^ and object of this joke? Its object is to bring ridicule and insult upon a teacher, upon one who takes the place, in a certain sense, of parents. Its result is to subject him to all manner of indignities, to cause a crowd of boys to scoff and» jeer at a man who, whatever his short-comv ings may have been, was still entitled to their respect and obedience."

"But, Mr. Middleton," ^ Harry Quip inquired, "how was it we didn't notice these things ourselves? We all thought it was

simply a funny story, and saw no great harm in it; now, of course, we see it differently."

"The reason is simple enough, Harry. The author quite cleverly smoothes over the real evil. In a counterfeit bill only a sharp and practiced eye can detect the fraud. Now that you are young, many things which are wrong may escape you in such a story. In fact, to analyze such a passage as I have just read supposes in a boy a power of reasoning which, as a rule, is developed later on in life. What is true of this book is true of thousands of the like publications. They are written in such a way as to catch the young imagination; but their effect in the long run is to cause boys unconsciously to admire what is ignoble and sinful. I have known boys to read these books for a time, and not be corrupted. But they were warned of the danger betimes. Such reading indulged in continually cannot fail of distorting all that is truly noble in the best disposition."

Mr. Middleton spoke at some length on this point. His words produced a decided effect. Richards and Sommers, in particular, entered into a solemn agreement between themselves to give up the dime-novel et id genus omne for good and all.

But the prefect's words effected even more. It set the boys to looking up good books; and here Percy proved himself of real service. The amount he had read was indeed great, and so careful had his mother been in the selection of his books that, bv <i certain acquired delicacy of taste, he could now detect what was vile in

juvenile literature, and perceive what was true and beautiful. He it was of the entire class who had understood at once the underlying baseness of the picnic story.

Under his direction, Tom, Harry, and a number of their classmates set about reading the choicest books for the young. So regular were they in their method that their proceedings were virtually equivalent to a junior literary academy. Of a cold December recreation-day, they would, with permission, assemble in a class-room, and discuss with pleasure and profit their readings. Even Richards' former misdirected pursuits in this line proved to be of some use. He brought up for discussion many of the incidents he had read, and, with the nobler ideals which their present course of reading and the prefect's instructions had given them, these young blue-stockings were quick to recognize the deformity of such writings.

In short, while Percy had been transformed by his friends into something of a true boy, with a true boy's love for out-door sports, they, in turn, following the law of action and reaction, had been transformed by him into lovers of books. He had received much, but had given more.

Since his first introduction to the reader, our little friend has changed not a little. His face has become fuller. But pretty as it formerly was in its delicacy and refinement, it is now beautiful in its rosy healthfulness. He is, if anything, a trifle stouter too. But his hands! Ah! Tom Playfair would now think twice before asking Percy to strike him straight from

the shoulder. Percy, under Tom's special direction and training, has been using boxing-gloves very regularly for several weeks, and, in addition, his hands have been hardened by continual exercise, his legs have been developed with much running; his whole constitution, in fact, has been built up and strengthened by plenty of open-air life. He is still the same little gentleman, but he is more.

A brook may run smoothly enough for a time; but it will surely come sooner or later upon obstacles. So life cannot slip by without troubles; even the best are not exempted.

Percy, just two days before Christmas, met with an adventure which came very nigh—
But let us give it the benefit of a separate chapter.

CHAPTER XVII

In which Percy Falls Foul of the Village Youth and is Compelled to "Run the Gauntlet"

I

T WAS a bright, clear, crisp afternoon in December, as three students with linked arms, and gayly facing the biting wind which brought a glow to their cheeks, set off at a swinging stride for the village of St. Maure's.

"Only two more days!" said Donnel. 'Yes," assented Keenan. "And then a great week of fun. There'll be a hard, solid frost to-night, I think; for it's getting colder all the time. If it keeps on this way, the thermometer will sneak down below freezing-point before seven this evening."

"Oh, I do hope so!" chimed in Percy, the third member of the cheerful party. "My skates have come, and I'm so anxious to try them."

"You have never done any skating yet, have you?" asked Keenan.

"Oh dear, no! How could I? My sisters couldn't teach me that, you know."

"Well, we'll see you through safely," said Donnel. "I can't see what use a boy has for winter if he can't skate."

"But I can slide," said Percy, modestly. "Still, I must confess I never did care much for winter."

"No wonder," Keenan remarked. "A boy

who can't throw snow-balls, or even make them, nor skate, nor go sleigh-riding, nor go hunting, can't have much cause for liking freezing weather. For my part, I much prefer winter to summer."

"Indeed! you don't say! You astonish me!" Percy exclaimed.

"So do I," put in Donnel. "Give me winter, knee-deep in snow. Give me the winter winds wearily sighing, as Tennyson has it; give me— well, to come down a little bit—give me a good pair of skates, and let me go flying along a frozen stretch of river, with the wind frolicking about my ears, and the frost trying for all it is worth to nip my nose, and I'm perfectly happy."

"And give me," said Keenan, u a clear, cold winter's night, with the moon and stars shining clear and keen—ever so much brighter than in summer. Then give me the ground covered with snow, and sparkling and twinkling in the fairy moonlight; then let me hear, rising upon the silence of the wintry night, the merry sleigh-jingles or some low, deep bell, and I feel a— well I feel just immense."

It should be remembered that our two friends are members of the poetry class. But Percy, though no poet, was by no means wanting in imagination.

"Indeed, George," he said softly, "I have often felt the beauty of such a scene as you speak of. But there is one memory which gives it a still greater charm and makes it more beautiful than any other scene. Whenever I have looked out of my window at home on such a night, another thought has always come to

my mind. The bleak trees, and the hills covered with snow, have brought back the country about Bethlehem. The bright stars have reminded me of the wonderful star that the Magi followed, and the sharp cold, the Infant Jesus, Who came to us in His love on just such a night."

"Honestly," said Donnel, "some like thought has often occurred to me—not so pretty as yours, though, Percy. And do you know, I really believe that winter, with all its bleakness and sterility, has come to be loved by thousands, not least by us boys, because around with it comes Christmas with all the love and joy and good feeling of that sacred and happy time."

"True," rejoined Keenan. "Do you remember that ode of Horace's on Winter, which we translated in class about a month ago?—

" 'Vides ut alta stet nive candidum Soracte, nee jam sustineant onus Sylvae laborantes, geluque Flumina constiterint acuto' —

I forget the rest. It is certainly a beautiful ode. But how little does it show of real love for winter! — Tile on the generous logs. Out with the yet more generous wine. Let's keep warm, and eat and drink, and enjoy ourselves by the hearth'—that's the idea of the whole ode. If Horace had but known the Christ as we do, what a grand poem he would have given us! Some of the most beautiful things

in art and literature are inspired by the memory of Christ's birth."

'Yes," said Percy, "like Milton's hymn on the Nativity, which I like very much, though I can't understand many parts of it. Then do you remember what Shakespeare says on this very subject?—

'Some say that ever 'gainst that season comes Wherein Our Saviour's birth is celebrated, The bird of dawning singeth all night long: And then, they say, no spirit dare stir

abroad; The nights are wholesome; then no planets

strike, No fairy takes, nor witch hath power to

charm, So hallowed and so gracious is the time.' "

"Well, Percy," said Donnel, "there'll be no standing you by the time you get as high as the poetry class. Even now you out-poet the poets. Where did you learn all your quotations?"

"Sister Jane, my oldest sister, used to point out passages for me to memorize."

"I wish I'd had a few sister Janes when I was young," said Keenan. "I'd know a little more.'

"I've got three sisters at home," added John. "But if ten sisters could do such great work with you, you wretched small boy, I really wish now that I had twenty-seven."

Percy answered with a laugh: "Ten are

very good, John, but twenty-seven might be too much of a good thing."

They were now walking along the principal street of the village.

"Well," added Percy, "I'll have to leave you now, if you're going up to the shoe-store first. I'm going in here to get some gloves and things. So good-by."

'Take care of yourself," answered Donnel. Percy entered a dry-goods store (in which butter, eggs, ploughs, watches, and flour were also sold), and made a few purchases. He then took a walk through the village, and, not meeting with George or John, concluded to return to the college alone.

He had not gone very far, when he descried further up the road a gathering of people near the house of one of the village doctors. His attention was at once engaged. What could be the matter?

The doctor's house in those days—and, for aught the writer knows, the doctor may still be there— stood quite alone, being distant some sixty rods or so from the body of the village. Percy, with all the eager curiosity of youth, hastened forward. As he drew nearer he discerned that the group, as far as could be seen, consisted entirely of boys, and that they were all strangers to him. Whatever might be the object that drew them together, it was clear that they were highly amused; for they were gazing intently at some person or thing at their feet, and jeering and laughing noisily.

Making his way through the motley group, Percy's eyes were greeted with a sight which moved him almost to tears. On the ground, in a state of stupid intoxication, lay a man in the prime of life, or little beyond it, his otherwise fine, intellectual face marred by the animal expression of one under the influence of mind-stealing liquor. Any one at all observant could see at a glance that he was not an habitual drinker. Beside him, crushed and battered, lay his hat. But sad as was his spectacle of degradation, it was raised to the pathetic by the presence of another element. Kneeling beside the man, and gazing earnestly into his face, was a pretty, well-dressed child of nine or ten, his eyes filled with tears, his cheeks pale with fright and awe, his whole countenance expressive of dismay and bitter surprise. It was the son gazing on the father's disgrace. The school-books, fallen heedlessly from his hands and lying scattered about on the ground, indicated that the child had been on his way home from the village school. The irreverent sur-rounders were mainly his fellow-students, theif numbers slightly swelled by several juvenile idlers of the village.

"Papa! papa!" the child was sobbing as Percy came up, "come home with me. Oh, dear papa, come home!"

It seemed hardly probable that the recumbent man was at all conscious of these words.

"Shake him up," suggested a rude voice.

'Your papa's pretty drunk, Johnny/' ejaculated another, unfeelingly.

"Turn the hose on him !" cried a would-be joker.

Percy's heart burned with indignation at

these coarse and brutal remarks; perhaps fof the first time in his life he clinched his fist with vexation.

But the poor little boy himself seemed to be entirely unconscious of these suggestions. He was alone in the world with his father; all else was forgotten.

"Oh, papa, papa!" he exclaimed in a piteous voice, "do speak to me! Are you sick, papa? Come home. It is too cold to lie here."

That these boys could laugh in the face of so bitter an experience to an innocent child may seem incredible. But such was the fact.

'Talk louder," counselled one of those un-painted savages; " perhaps the old man's deaf."

"Pull his hair, why don't you?" added a burly fellow of coarse features, who, by his swagger and general air, seemed to be a leader among the village youth.

'That's sensible advice, Buck; give him a little more of it," said a smaller ruffian, addressing the last speaker.

"Here, I'll wake him," said the individual styled Buck; and advancing, he took the man by the shoulders and shook him rudely.

The weeping child sprang to his feet, his dark eyes flashing.

"Let him alone !" he cried passionately. "He is my father. You mustn't touch him." He gave the fellow a stout push.

"I don't care whose father he is," said the callous young ruffian. "Come on, old man, wake up!"

The little lad became furious with rage. He

caught Buck with one hand, and with the other •:ried to beat him off.

"Oh dear, dear!" cried Percy, unable to be silent any longer, and breaking through the crowd. "This is too sad. You ought to be ashamed of yourself, sir," he said, his blue eyes flashing with indignation, as he addressed the rude fellow. "If you don't respect the man, you might at least spare the feelings of the boy."

Buck, heedless of the blows rained upon him by the angry child, released his hold and started back in surprise. Even the boy desisted from his attack, and turned to look in silence upon his defender. The crowd for a moment became breathless with astonishment. That a slight, fair-faced college-boy, almost girlish in form and feature, should make bold to reprimand Buck, the terror of every village-lad, was too much for their slender and poorly developed imaginations. But astonishment soon gave way to indignation, derision, and contempt.

"Oh my! what a dude!" "Go home to your mamma." "He's a college dandy." "Who let you loose?" These and a number of rude jests and exclamations were bandied from mouth to mouth; while gentle Percy, his bosom heaving with pitying emotion, stood, in the strength of his indignation, fearless and unabashed, boldly facing the burly leader.

Buck, his face purple with rage, raised his hand as a signal for quiet.

'You little fool," he growled, "what do you mean by speaking to me that way?"

Percy placed himself between Buck and the

man.

u

I can't bear it; I really can't," he protested. "It should move a heart of stone to see a poor boy in this sad condition. And you boys come around him, and laugh and make fun. Oh, it is cowardly!"

"Cowardly!" echoed Buck.

"It is; it is."

The bully struck Percy a heavy blow with his open palm. Percy fell, but arose quickly, his mouth bleeding.

"You may strike and strike," he said, in a low firm tone. "But I say it is cowardly. It is lit is!"

All had now forgotten the drunken man. Even the child standing beside his father turned from his own great trouble, and stood gazing upon Percy in astonishment—and love. Of all the many eyes fixed upon our hero, his were the only ones which expressed the least sympathy.

A boy of about Percy's height, though somewhat stouter, now stepped from the crowd.

"You said we were cowards," he snarled. "I'm your size. Do you want to fight?"

"No, indeedy! I don't believe in fighting. Oh, but please do leave this poor man alone. You know it's cowardly to insult a helpless man in the presence of his son."

There was a moment of indecision.

"Let's make him run the gauntlet!" shouted one.

There followed a general chorus of assent; and Buck immediately seized Percy, who, ignorant of the nature of running the gauntlet, made little or no struggle. But the little boy could not bear to see his champion thus treated. He rushed forward and threw his arms about Percy.

"Help, help!" he shouted at the top of his voice.

"Shut up, you little sneak!" growled Buck, vainly trying to disengage the child from his hold on Percy's body. "Here, some of you fellows, pull this chap off."

The child was quickly, rudely torn away, and Percy was left in the cruel grasp of his captor. In less time than it takes to tell it, the boys closed together in a double line, facing one another, and with just a little space between. Through these two lines Percy was to make his way, receiving, as he passed, cuffs, kicks, and such indignities as each of these cruel boys had the power and opportunity of inflicting.

"Now," said Buck, bringing him to the opening at one end of the rank, "run right through as fast as you can."

Percy had no knowledge whatever of "running the gauntlet." Poor boy! the vile tricks of the ruder class of youth were as yet unknown to him. So he stood irresolute. But a rude push from the leader sent him stumbling in between the boys. He was at once greeted with kicks and blows from those who were nearest; and the delicate boy almost immediately fell flat to the earth. No sooner had he fallen, however, than one of the roughs raised him and pushed him on. A few steps farther and he Jell again, dazed and almost stunned. He was

h

mercilessly forced to his feet, and the disgraceful violence renewed.

Suddenly a loud shout arose, and as Percy fell to the ground for the third time, two o£ his persecutors measured their length beside him. Donnel and Keenan had come to the rescue.

CHAPTER XVIII

In which Some of our Friends Find it Neces* sary to Fight — Also to Run

Co engrossed had these wretches been in their cruel sport that our two friends, Donnel, the largest and best developed boy of the small yard, and Keenan, the quickest, hardiest, and most wiry, were upon them and among them before they had the least idea that an enemy was approaching. Percy's two friends (who had heard the little lad's shout for help) came upon the scene at a dead run; and such added impetus did they bring to bear on the young miscreants that, as they dashed into the crowd, they sent five or six sprawling to the ground. Nor did they give the astonished town-boys time or opportunity to recover themselves. Both, though famous among their fellow-stu» dents as peace-lovers and peace-makers, were, for all that, excellent boxers. So, without stopping to make any inquiries, or to count the number of their slain, they followed up their first onslaught by raining blows right and left upon Percy's tormentors.

In an instant there came a panic upon the crowd. It was highly increased when some one shouted: —

"Look out, fellows! there's a big crowd of college-boys coming."

This was too much for the general bravery.

There was a lively scattering in all directions. But the victory was by no means complete. Buck, the pride and glory of a hundred village encounters, had a reputation at stake; and giving no ear to this warning, he addressed himself to John Donnel, who had already introduced himself, as it were, to Mr. Buck by giving that hero of a hundred village encounters a decidedly unpleasant rap over the eyes.

"Time, there, will you?" cried Buck. "Just give me time to get off my coat, and then I'll teach you a thing or two."

"I'll give you time to take off your whole wardrobe!" bawled John Donnel, the most peaceable and good-natured student in St. Maure's College.

While this interchange of civilities was going on, and the rough was whipping off his coat, George Keenan was busily attending to a short, thick-set, sandy-faced boy, who, second only to Buck in local fame, had held his ground along with his chieftain.

But Keenan's stunted form and slight build sadly deceived his opponent. That wiry, under-grown lad, with all the quickness and lightness of a cat, possessed in addition the strength of iron muscles. The second hero of the village started in with the openly expressed intention of "annihilating" Keenan. But so quick and fast did the blows come from George's fists that very soon he was fain to stand almost entirely upon the defensive. And he found presently that he was ill able to do even this. With every third or fourth blow, George broke through his guard. Presently the second bulty.

of the village, who "looked the whole world in the face, for he feared not any boy" (except Buck, of course), began to move slowly backwards, endeavoring by this retrogression to keep the blows from his face. Keenan was by nature of a phlegmatic disposition, but his appearance and conduct on this occasion would hardly lead a spectator to suspect the slightest existence of any such negative quality in him. His cheeks were flushed, his eyes ablaze; and, as his opponent began to step back, he rushed upon him with ever-increasing heat and energy. Blow upon blow breaking through the fellow's guard sent him reeling from side to side. Harder and harder Keenan pushed him. The bully was losing heart. His lips had became puffy; his eyes were swelling fast; and soon he was unable to keep up even the pretence of a guard. Every blow now told on him, and he was obliged to yield ground more rapidly. He was soon close upon a tree, which, not having eyes at the back of his head, he could not, of course, perceive, and just as he had backed within two feet of it, George succeeded in dealing him a tremendous blow between the eyes — a blow which sent the back of the village hero's head with a resounding whack against the tree. This was too much for the village hero. With a roar of pain, he turned tail and fled towards his dismayed companions, who had again gathered together, but at a safe and very respectable distance.

All this took place in not more than two minutes' time; and George, coolly adjusting his cuffs and smoothing down his hair, turned back to rejoin his friends. The scene had changed somewhat. The drunken man was now in a sitting posture, gazing about with a mixed expression of stupidity and surprise. His child, standing by his side, was watching the actions of John Donnel and Buck, who, at a little distance from Percy, were sparring warily. Percy, his clothes torn and soiled, had arisen, and was wiping the blood from his mouth. George hastened forward to watch the issue of the contest.

"Hadn't you better hold on?" said John to his opponent. "Your side have all gone. I don't care about fighting."

The answer to this was a blow on the face, which the bully, seeing John off his guard, contrived to get in.

John had relieved his conscience. It was now a question of defence.

"Keep steady, John," counselled Keenan. "Have a lookout for some mean trick. I wouldn't trust that fellow."

John was steady enough. No one since his first appearance at college had ever known him to be concerned in a fight; but it was not from fear, for he was indeed a most scientific boxer, When he and Keenan put on the gloves in the college playroom for a friendly bout, they were always surrounded by an admiring crowd, who, as a rule, were well repaid for their attention.

But on this occasion his opponent was not to be despised. Stouter and larger and older than John, he was also the stronger. It was a question of very great skill and inferior strength against great skill and superior strength. As

for Buck, he had no doubts concerning the result.

For some time the sparring continued, wary on both sides. Several times Buck assumed the offensive ; but he succeeded poorly in breaking John's guard. One of his attempts, indeed, resulted to his disadvantage. Before he could recover himself after a vigorous lunge, John caught him sharply behind the ear. Buck's con-fidence weakened, but his rage grew proportionately stronger, and expressed itself in a most villainous expression of countenance.

"Look out for the finger-trick, John," said George, in a voice so low as to be heard by Donnel alone. "If I can judge by the way that fellow's acting, he's going to try it on you. Shut your mouth tight.

Did John understand this hint of George's? It would appear that he did not, for he kept his mouth still slightly open, and even appeared to open it wider. And George was correct in his suspicions. Buck, seeing his opportunity, suddenly caught the left hand of John with his own left, and with the right tried to find his mouth. But John had heard and understood Keenan's hint. His mouth was at once closed tight, and before the vile trickster could recover his position, he planted two very telling blows on his face, one of them taking an eye.

The village hero of a hundred fights was somewhat disheartened. For the first time in years, he had met an opponent superior in skill to himself. He was now, moreover, at a disadvantage. His vision was no longer clear, and it was in vain he endeavored to keep track of

John's rapid and aggressive movements. But he had one chance yet of coming out with honor. He believed, and with truth (for he was the stronger and the heavier set), that if he could close with his adversary, the battle might yet be his. He drew back, therefore, little by little, intending at some favorable moment to rush in upon John. But Keenan, who kept his wits perfectly clear, perceived his intention.

"Keep your eyes open, John," he whispered. "He's going to close in on you."

A moment later, Buck, suddenly drawing back a few feet, made a savage, tiger-like spring at Donnel. But the most peace-loving student of St. Maure's had been awaiting^and expecting this movement. He jumped quickly to one side, and as Buck passed by him, he dealt him a full, vigorous blow upon the ear, which sent the bully forwards at such an increased rate of speed that he lost his balance and fell heavily to the earth.

A howl of rage and dismay arose from the fallen hero's sympathizers, who, however, still maintained their respectful distance. The strain on their already strained imaginations at seeing the village leader lying at the feet of a smaller boy — and a college-boy at that —was overpowering. And then their idol seemed in nc hurry to vindicate himself. He lay prone upon the ground, and, if one could judge by his actions, had his doubts about the propriety or advisability of arising.

But the crowd had now recovered in some measure from their first panic. After all, it was not a party of college-boys, as they had

been led to suppose, but only two students who had taken the field. One spirited youth, under a growing sense of security, stooped and picked up a stone. His example was at once followed by several.

"John! Percy!" said Keenan, who was as cool as ever, "we've got to run for it; I think those fellows are going to stone us."

"Let them come on, the cowards!" said John. "Two can play at that game. I wouldn't run from them if they were a thousand."

"But think of Percy," pleaded George. "He's too delicate for this kind of amusement. It may be healthy enough for you and me. But don't be selfish; we must consider him."

John's common-sense asserted itself.

"You're right: we must save him. Come on, Percy."

Percy during the progress of the fight, had been praying for his friends with all the earnestness and confidence of his pure and loving spirit.

"Don't mmd me," he said. ;< Save yourselves, John and George; I'll stay."

"You must be crazy," said John.

"No, Fm not. Oh, please go. You'll get hurt."

"Oh," said Keenan, "he's hurt his leg again. Did you ever hear of such legs?"

George had a keen sense of observation. Percy's ankle had been hurt in a fall, but he had made every effort to conceal his trouble from his two allies.

Even as Keenan made this announcement, a stone whistled by Donnel's head.

Donnel made a rush to catch up Percy; but Keenan was before him.

"No, you don't, John," he said, as he swung Percy into his arms and set off at a run; "you're pretty well blown already, and I'm quite fresh."

Scarcely had they begun their flight towards the college, when a yell of rage flew up from the crowd—who had thus far kept their distance—followed by a shower of stones. It was really refreshing to see how lightly George sped along the road with his burden. His height and figure were beyond doubt very deceptive. Compared with lads of his own size, it might be said of him almost literally that "his strength was as the strength of ten."

"Oh, George," said Percy, "you'll be hurt on my account. Please let me down. I'm not afraid; and I think I can run a little."

"Keep quiet, you young John L.," George made answer. "This is just fun for me. Why, I can run near a mile with twenty pounds of dumb-bell, and you're not much worse; and besides, I haven't to run half so far."

In truth, one beholding George's face and expression might have judged that he was indulging in a mad romp.

The crowd behind were now in full chase, and of course were gaining on our runners.

"I say," said John, who was taking it quite easy, so as not to outstrip George, "they're getting too close; and I've got the most brilliant kind of an idea, and we ought both of us to be ashamed it didn't occur to us before. Let me hold part of Percy. Suppose I take his legs, for instajige."

The suggestion was good and timely. To use George's phrase, they "divided Percy up, M and then set forward at much increased speed.

This change was greeted by another howl of rage from the pursuers, and another shower of stones, one or which struck George below the knee.

"Good shot!" exclaimed George. "My legs are the toughest part of me. Cheer up, Percy, we're getting close to the college. We'll be at the bridge crossing College Creek in two minutes. Brace up, my boy; you'll live to run away again."

"I'm not at all afraid," said Percy, with his beautiful smile, and fixing eyes full of confidence and gratitude upon his brave deliverers. "I know that I'm in good company."

"George," cried Donnel, suddenly, "aren't there two of our fellows walking along by Brown's Hotel just beyond the bridge?"

The crowd behind had so gained that matters threatened to come to a crisis. Another shower of stones might prove to be very dangerous.

George's keen eyes strained themselves in the direction to which John had called his attention. As he looked, his face changed from doubt to delight.

"Hurrah!" he said, "it's Ryan and McNeff."

There was magic in the word Ryan. Who. then, was Ryan? He was the stoutest and bravest young man in the large yard, with the additional glory of being the patriarch-student of St. Maure's. Naturally hot-tempered, and, in consequence, very troublesome to his prefects - during his first and second years at college, he

had in time succeeded so far in curbing his quarrelsome disposition as to use his physical powers only in self-defence or in helping the weak.

"Ryan! Ryan!" shouted John and George together.

"Oh, pshaw! he doesn't hear us."

Suddenly a loud, shrill, piercing noise rent the air. Percy, most luckily, had been cherishing Mr. Middleton's whistle as a sort of relic and keepsake.

Ryan and McNeff turned about at once, and immediately came down the road at full speed.

It might be mentioned here that the new champion, Ryan, was better known in the village than any living person not actually residing therein; and, especially in his earlier days, had frequently taught the village-boys many lessons not to be learned from books.

His appearance was enough. Stones dropped from hands just raised to throw them; and every mother's son of the pursuers wheeled about, and made with all earnestness for home.

"Hurrah!" shouted Keenan, as he and John reached the bridge and rested themselves against its railings, "the victory's ours. Cock-a-doodle-do !" And he gave a novel and unique imitation of a hoarse rooster with an abnormal and remarkably uncommon crow.

"Never say die!" exclaimed Percy, getting upon his feet.

"And," added Donnel, "we'll live to fight another day, because we had sense enough to run away."

CHAPTER XIX

Beginning of the Christmas Holidays. Percy is Called to the Parlor

" \V ELL >" sa ^ Ry an » as ne g a ' me(i the bridge much in advance of McNeff, U I thought you belonged to the peace-party. But you look as though you had been knocking out the small-fry of the village by contract. What's happened?"

"It seems, " Donnel made answer, "that Percy left the village several minutes before us, and took it into his head to break up a meeting of some twenty or thirty roughs."

"I only told them to go away," said Percy. "They were making fun of a little boy whose father was lying on the ground — and, would you believe it? I think the man was actually drunk — so drunk that he couldn't walk. I never saw any such thing before outside of a book. But the whole thing was so cruel. I had to speak out; I couldn't help myself."

"Yes; and they'd have spoiled his chances of enjoying the Christmas holidays if we hadn't come up. You see, Ryan, they were making him run the gauntlet."

"Oh, the brutes!" exclaimed Ryan in great indignation. "Percy, you're the knight "sans peur.' But what's the matter with your hand?"

"I think a stone must have struck it," said Percy, holding it up. "Oh dear! it's bleeding, too/

"It's about time for you to notice it." And Ryan, taking a handkerchief from his pocket, wrapped it about Percy's bleeding fingers. "And your mouth is swollen, also," he added, "and there are marks of blood about it—and then you've a stiff ankle. Good gracious! you look uglier than myself, which is saying a great deal. Here, boys, bring him up to the college, and induce the infirmarian to put him into plasters, or he'll come to pieces. If he's attended to now, he'll be all right for Christmas. Donnel, your face is cut a little."

"Oh, I enjoy having my face cut above, all things. I was just on the point of asking some one to cut it for me, when a big village tough by the name of Buck, seeing my desire, kindly obliged me. Yes," he added merrily, "I now want only one thing to complete my happiness — and that's a black eye."

"But, Mr. Ryan," put in Percy with all earnestness, "I'm so anxious about that little boy and his father. Those mean boys may return on them."

"I'll bet they don't stay long, then," said Ryan, decidedly. 'You just go home, Percy, and swallow all the medicine the Brother will give you. McNeff and myself will see the man home safely, if we have to carry him."

With this promise Percy was thoroughly satisfied; and Ryan, having learnt the whereabouts of the drunken man, set off at a pace which, giving it the most dignified expression allowable, might be called very fast walking, fully determined to carry out his promise, even should he bring the whole village about his ears.

It may be added that he had no difficulty in putting his promise into effect.

The following day was December the twenty-third. In the afternoon the closing exercises of the year were held in the college study-hall. After an overture from the college orchestra, the "testimonials of excellent deportment," or "conduct-cards," were distributed. The names of the boys meriting this honor were read out in alphabetical order. When John Donnel advanced to the platform to receive his card from the hands of the president, his face, very much out of shape — u Lob-sided, isn't It?" whispered Tom to Harry Quip— there was so vigorous a clapping of hands that Donnel blushed. Kee-nan's appearance elicited a no less hearty applause. But when Percy Wynn, the last on the list, advanced to the platform, his face dotted with sticking-plaster, his hand bandaged, and with a perceptible limp, there arose such a cheer as had never before startled the echoes of the hall. Cheering in any room of the college was, of course, against all rule. But the president was not over-mathematical: he could make allowances. Indeed he afterwards remarked, it was said, that he felt tempted to join in himself. As for the prefects, the guardians of order, not one of them made so much as a gesture of disapproval. Nay, more: several of the boys afterwards asserted that Mr. Middle-ton had himself taken an active part in the applause ; but this, I take it, was an exaggeration.

The boys readily accepted it as a fact, however, and liked their prefect the more for it.

That Percy was fully up in his studies was evidenced by his class-standing. In English composition he was first, Richards second; in arithmetic, Tom first, Percy second; English grammar, Quip, Playfair and Wynn equal; Greek, Wynn and Playfair equal; in Latin, Wynn first, Playfair second.

Tom shook his fist at Percy. 'You plastered-up pugilist," he whispered; "next time I teach you any Latin, it will be a very cold day, and you'll have to whistle!"

"You'll have to teach me how to whistle first, Tom."

"Not if I know myself," replied the humbled ex-professor. "I don't care about seeing you beat me at that, too."

But for all this, Tom was proud of the success of his pupil. As a slight expression of his overcharged feelings, he was known to have turned several handsprings in private; and he went about during the day, speaking of Percy as a "crippled pupil of his, who had had the impudence to beat his professor." It was the first time in a year that Tom had missed the monthly Latin medal, but he was far more gratified at Percy's earning it than he had ever been at his own success. His was too large a heart to be disturbed by petty jealousy.

The premiums all distributed to the leaders of the various classes, the college choir came forward with a pretty Christmas hymn, consisting of solo and chorus. Percy had the solo. The exhilaration of the time and place, the

Christmas emotions throbbing in the hearts of his audience, the warm feelings which the kindly demonstrations of the students had awakened in his bosom—all combined to raise Percy to such a state of exaltation that the glory and peace of that Christmas night of long ago seemed to find echo in his silvery voice. The chorus, too, animated by the fine spirit Percy had evoked, sang with a tenderness and feeling far above their ordinary efforts.

When the song was concluded, there was scarcely any applause. The religious element in its sweetest and most charming form had been touched, and the enthusiasm of it was expressed in reverential silence.

The president then made a few remarks, ending with cordial wishes for a merry Christmas to all; and presently the boys, freed from their books, were hard at it, chasing the wayward foot-ball.

Percy, in his maimed condition, was unable to join them in this sport. So he and Tom repaired to the playroom. Just as they were finishing a game of checkers, a boy came running in, with—

"Oh, I say, Percy; you're wanted in the parlor."

"Goodness! perhaps it's my mamma! Oh, it's too bad!"

'Well, you're a nice, affectionate son! The idea of beginning to growl at the prospect of seeing your mother!" said Tom, with his most serious expression.

'You know what I mean, Tom. She'll be shocked at seeing me w sticking-plasters,"

"Oh, I wouldn't bother," said Tom. "You look just immense behind a sticking-plaster. If I were you, I'd wear one all the time for ornament. You might make it fashionable. It looks every bit as sensible as wearing a bang, anyhow."

'Well, I don't care about starting the fashion on mamma first. But perhaps it's some one else. In her last letter, she wrote that she wouldn't be here before the first of January. Do you think it can be my mamma, Tom?"

"If I were you, I'd go and find out," said the malicious professor of Latin. "You might tell her that I intend to put in a bill for teaching you, with interest at ten per cent."

Percy made a few hasty changes in his toilet, and hurried over to the parlor.

It was with trembling hand he turned the door-knob. He hesitated even then for a moment before throwing open the door. But his anxiety was at once dissipated. No mamma was there, expecting to see her darling child the picture of health, freshness, and vigor. Seated beside the president of the college was a strange gentleman, his hand clasped in affectionate familiarity by a little boy, who released his clasp as Percy entered, and ran eagerly forward to meet him. Percy had no difficulty in recognizing the child as his little friend of the previous day's adventure. But he could hardly bring himself to believe that the stately dignified gentleman before him was the drunkard of the village common.

CHAPTER XX

Introduces an Extraordinary New-comer to Percy and the Reader

*"pHE gentleman rose, somewhat awkwardly it must be admitted, as Percy entered.

"Percy," said the president, "this is Mr. Burdock."

Percy made his inimitable bow.

"Mr. Burdock," he said, his face suffused with blushes, "I am happy to make your acquaintance."

The gentleman shook his hand warmly, and the accompanying look expressed his gratitude more than any number of fine phrases.

There was a slight pause, a pause that promised to become oppressive. But here the child came bravely to the rescue.

"Oh, I say, Percy, you and me don't have to be—what do you call it—"

"Introduced." suggested Percy.

"That's the word; I couldn't get it, it's so long. My name's Frank, and I like you like anything."

This novel avowal set the whole party laughing, and relieved the awkwardness which, naturally enough, Mr. Burdock felt in the presence of his beardless boy-defender.

Frank, during the laugh, was shaking Percy's hand, and derived such supreme enjoyment from this very simple performance that he kept it up for over a minute.

"Percy," said Mr. Burdock at length, "I must confess that I feel somewhat embarrassed just now. But I thank you from my heart for the lesson you have unconsciously taught me. People say that I am a scholar, that I give much of my time to books; but I don't mind telling you in the presence of your president that I have learned from you many things more beautiful than my best writers have taught me. To-morrow I leave St. Maure's for good."

"I'm sorry you're going, sir," said Percy, "for I hoped to see more of Frank."

Upon this, Frank seized Percy's hand again, and shook it warmly.

"I'm glad to hear that," said Mr. Burdock, smiling.

"And so am I," said the little fellow, still shaking Percy's hand, "for I'm going to stay with you, Percy. Papa is going to let me be a boarder."

"Oh, indeed! I'm so glad!"

"Nothing would do Frank, after what hap. pened yesterday," put in Mr. Burdock, "but to come to school at St. Maure's College. This was rather hard on me," he added, turning to the president with a smile; "for I've spent the last ten years in abusing religion in general, and Catholicity with Catholic training in particular. But I have changed all that the last twenty-four hours. Percy, and two friends who came to his assistance, have levelled all my objections. By the way, where are those two boys, Percy?"

'I think they are gone walking, sir." 'Well, I hope to see them some day, and

thank them. And now, reverend Father, there's one other point I should have touched upon. My boy has no religion."

"Oh !" exclaimed Percy, unable to conceal his dismay.

"But my ideas," continued Mr. Burdock, "are changed on that subject, too. If Frank desires, he may now choose for himself."

"Have you got religion, Percy?" asked Frank, gravely.

"Oh, yes, indeed!"

"Well, then, papa, I want to get Percy's religion.
c<
No matter whether it's right or wrong?" asked the father.

This puzzled little Frank for a moment, but he brightened as he made answer: "Oh, I'm sure it's right. If it can make a boy be as nice and kind and brave as Percy, it can't be very wrong. Don't you think that's a fact, papa? '

"Well, no matter; you may choose for yourself, Frank. But try to understand what you are choosing, and why."

"You may be sure," said the president, gravely, "that he will not become a Catholic unless he really desires it; not then, even, unless he fully believes those truths which we hold necessary."

"I trust you fully, reverend Father. Now, Frank, as I wish to have some talk in private with the president, I shall leave you in Percy's hands."

"Come on, Frank," said Percy. "I'll show you the yard and everything. Good-by, Mr. Burdock."

"Good-by, my boy. Again let me thank you: you have done me more service than you can realize. You are one of nature's noblemen."

"Oh dear me!" exclaimed Percy. "You're quite welcome, I'm sure, but it isn't worth mentioning."

"That's what you say. Now, Frank, my little boy, good-by"— he raised Frank in his arms and kissed him fondly—"and—eh—eh— God bless you."

It was with difficulty the strong man uttered these words, and his voice trembled as he spoke.

"He's my child—my only child," he added, turning away and bowing his head. "My only child—and his mother is dead."

Every word of this utterance told a tale of tears and of years of abiding sorrow and love.

"Oh, poor Frank!" cried Percy, his eyes melting with pity. "Come away, Frank; your papa will become only more sad if you remain longer."

As the door shut them from the room, Frank broke into sobs.

"That's right, Frank; have a good cry," said Percy, sympathetically. "I can easily imagine how sad it is to part from so kind a father."

"Oh, he always was so good and so kind to me!" sobbed the child. "He never spoke an unkind word to me. Oh, papa! papa!"

Percy was all sympathy and love. Scarcely fourteen himself, and but little more than a child among those of his own age at St. Maure's, he from that time took upon himself the office of protector to Frank.

"I am sure your papa is good. I can see it," he said. "I like him ever so much myself. And I noticed, too, how very sorry he was to leave you."

"And—and — did you hear what he said?" inquired Frank, eagerly, as he checked his sobs.

"What was that?"

"He said 'God bless you.' "

Percy was puzzled.

"I never heard him use that sort of talk before," continued Frank.

'What! You don't say so!" Percy was more astonished than words or looks could express. The idea that the simple phrase, "God bless you," should be a novelty to any one was to him something almost inconceivable. He paused at the lower end of the hall—they had thus far been walking along slowly — and kindly brushed the tears from Frank's cheek.

Frank Burdock could hardly be ten years old. He was small even for that age, and quite slightly made. While his features were regular, they were not of that faultless order wherein every lineament is so striking that nothing strikes. On the contrary, his forehead and deep chestnut eyes were worthy of more than a passing glance. Looking at these features, one could see that he united to the simplicity of the child the quiet, serious, thoughtful expression so rare in one of his years. His face, indeed, was eminently intellectual. Now a boy of ten with an intellectual face is something unusual. Frank was an unusual boy.

His training, it is worthy of remark, had been abnormal. Before he was well able toi

>

walk he had lost his mother; and to educate this only child, this dear relic of an intense affection, the surviving parent had devotedly set himself. But Mr. Burdock, unhappily, had for years previous been a pronounced infidel. And so, while carefully instructing Frank in such branches of secular learning as were fitted for a child not yet in his teens, he had entirely neglected the religious element. Frank's code of morality was, "Love your father and love your friends." To him the words/'God," "religion," "virtue," were almost meaningless. What such a course of instruction would ultimately had led to, it is unpleasant to speculate upon. But, happily for himself, Frank was as yet undeveloped; his passions had not gained their strength.

While the sorrows of a child are indeed poignant, they have this redeeming feature, that they pass quickly; and so when Percy conducted Frank to the small yard, some few minutes after the leave-taking between father and son, the little fellow had become quite tranquil.

"Now," said Percy, "I'm going to introduce you to some of my friends. They are all the nicest kind of boys. There's Tom Playfair, standing by the parallel bars. We must have a talk with him. Tom, I think, is one of the best boys living."

"He isn't any better than you, Percy, is he?"

"Oh yes, indeed ! He's worth a hundred like me," answered Percy, sincerely.

"I don't think so," Frank made answer, and giving out each word with great deliberation; "and I won't believe it till it's proved. Papa

says we're not to believe things till they are proved."

Percy laughed, as he conducted Frank over to Tom.

'Tom, here's a new boy. Allow me to introduce you to Frank Burdock."

"Happy Christmas, Frank," said Tom, shaking the new-comer's hand. "Seems to me I've seen you before."

"Maybe you did. I used to go to school up-

town."

"Oh, you did, did you? I reckon I must have run up against you when I was up-town buying shoes. I wear out a pair sometimes in two weeks. It takes Percy about six years. Well, I hope you'll like St. Maure's."

"I'm sure I will. Percy, here, and Donnel and Keenan— I think that's their names—are splendid boys."

"Oh," said Tom, recognizing in Frank the little boy whose cause Percy had championed, "I think you'll like the boys here better than the boys you used to go to school with."

At these words, Frank's eyes flashed, while his whole countenance darkened.

'The boys in the village school! I hate them P : He stamped his foot on the ground, and his delicate frame trembled with passion.

'Why, Frank," said Percy, "you must be joking."

"What!" exclaimed Frank. "Don't you hate them?"

"Indeed, no."

It was Frank's turn to be astonished.

"Not after the mean way they treated you?"

u We should never allow ourselves to hate people," said Percy in gentle accents. "And besides, those poor fellows may not have been taught better."

"I don't care," answered Frank, clinching his fists and speaking with much excitement; "they ought to know better, anyhow. And if I had a gun I'd—I'd shoot that big ugly Buck. I would, sure."

"Oh, you young blood-and-thunder!" exclaimed Tom, laughing, "you'll change your mind before you're much older."

"But I won't. I wish Buck and every one of those roughs were dead—yes, and buried, too. And I wouldn't want them to have any tombstones either, and nothing but an old wooden coffin. I hate 'em. I hate all people who treat me or my papa mean. And I love everybody who loves us." Here his face and tone softened, and he glanced affectionately at Percy.

"But it's wrong to hate," Percy said by way of answer to his glance.

"And do you know, old fellow," said Tom with much gravity, "that you're an out-and-out Jew, and no Christian at all? You want an eye for an eye."

"Oh, Tom," broke in Percy, opening his eyes very wide, and speaking with great earnestness and solemnity, lest Tom should think he was joking, "he doesn't know a thing about religion!"

Tom whistled, braced himself by spreading out his feet very wide, and thrusting his hands deep into his pockets.

"That's so." assented Frank; "but I'm going

PERCY WYNN

205

«o get a religion like Percy's. Have you got the same kind as Percy's, Tom?"

"Well," rejoined Tom, coolly, "I believe it's pretty much of the same kind of make. But I say, Frank, do you know what Christmas means?"

"Oh yes; it's a great day for presents and a big dinner with turkey and cranberry sauce and plum-pudding."

"Oh, you young heathen !"

Frank's eyes expressed perplexity, 'What's that, Tom?" he asked.

Percy laughed, as he said: 'Well, Frank, would you like to know what Christmas really is?"

"I want to know everything you know," Frank made answer with much gravity.

"Good boy, Frank!" said Tom, clapping him on the back. 'You're going in for a liberal education, and no mistake. But suppose, Percy, we go over to the chapel and show him the crib first; and while we're going there you can tell him all about Christmas."

The two made for the chapel, and on the way thither, Frank listened with no little interest and surprise to the account of the Christ-child's birth. In the chapel he gazed long and intently upon the pretty Christmas crib which had just been set up, and his features evinced that he was both delighted and impressed.

"Look," whispered Percy, pointing to the waxen figure of the Divine Babe. "Do you know what became of Him?"

"What, Percy?"

"In the end, He gave Himself up to suffer a cruel death for the sake of His enemies."

Frank gazed and pondered.

"Say, boys," he said presently, catching the hands of Percy and Tom, "if I say anything very queer now and then, you won't mind me, will you ? I don't want to say anything against your religion."

"You're changing already, old fellow," said Tom as they stepped out of the chapel. 'You're neither a Jew nor a heathen; you're yourself and nobody else., Halloa! here's Mr. Middleton. You must make his acquaintance, old boy; for he's to be your prefect."

But before Tom could go through the formalities of an introduction, Mr. Middleton assumed the initiative himself.

"Why, isn't this Frank Burdock?" he exclaimed, catching Frank's hand in all cordiality. 'I'm glad to see you. You're in my yard, you know; and I hope you'll feel at home from the start."

Frank gazed up into the kind face of the prefect.

"I hope so, too," he assented. "Mr. Middle-ton, why do you wear a gown?"

"I don't like to dress like ordinary people. But you'll understand these things better by and by. Percy, attend to Frank during supper; he may sit next to you. Afterwards bring him to me; I want to give him his place in the study-hall and dormitory."

And Mr. Middleton departed.

"He's a nice man," was Frank's comment, "even if he does like to dress funny. I like his face, too. He doesn't seem to be very rich, does he?"

"Oho! you're a Jew sure enough," said Tom. "But what makes you think him poor?"

"That old gown he had on. It ought to be black, I suppose, but it was green in spots; and then the thing he ties it round his waist with looks like —well, it looks something like going to seed."

"You're right, Frank," said Tom. "He is poor; he hasn't a cent in the world."

"He must spend his money as fast as he earns it then."

"He doesn't earn any money: he works for nothing."

A look of displeasure expressed itself upon the features of Frank.

"You're teasing me," he said, and turned away towards Percy.

"No, he isn't," said Percy. "It's quite true. Mr. Middleton doesn't receive one cent of salary '

"Is he crazy?"

"Oh dear, no! He's working for the love of God."

The expression on Frank's countenance at this announcement was one of infinite perplexity. He shut his eyes and pondered deeply. But his imagination seemed to be inadequate to the strong call made upon it.

"Let's take a run out in the fresh air," he suggested.

"Certainly," assented the two.^

They had scarcely gained their playground, when Frank, who had been looking about eager-

ly, suddenly brightened, and clapped his hands. "Look! there they are!" And he ran forward to greet Donnel and Keenan. "Oh, how do you do? I'm so glad to see you again! I go to school here, too, and my name's Frank Burdock."

"How are you, yourself?" answered John, swinging the little fellow into the air. 'You see, I want to take a good look at you; that's why I'm holding you up to the light. I'm John Donnel."

"And I'm George Keenan," said the other, catching Frank by the legs and bringing him to earth again.

For several moments Frank looked at George and John, as though something very heavy was weighing upon his youthful bosom. At length he spoke.

"Are you two in a higher class than Percy and Tom?"

"We are," answered both solemnly.

"Well, then, I want to ask you a question. 11

"Is it very hard?" asked John.

"No. Don't you hate Buck?"

"Certainly not," answered John.

"Suppose he were drowning in the river," continued Frank with an air of anxiety, "would you jump in to save him?"

"Well, if I thought I had a fair chance to save his life, I certainly would."

"You would?"

"Yes. What would you do?"

Frank's eyes flashed.

"I'd throw a brickbat at him I*'

CHAPTER XXI

In which Frank Asks a Great Many People a Great Many Questions; Teaches Percy How to "Strike Out" and Makes a Christmas, Speech Before Breakfast

""PHE morning of Christmas Eve—clear *nd cold. The sun, now risen with undimmed lustre, was making a million diamonds sparkle from frosted tree, from stunted grass, and from frozen earth. The boys, as they came running from the refectory to their yard, evinced unwonted animal spirits. The river, they were sure, was fit for skating.

While Percy was stooping over his box in the wash-room, looking up his skates, Frank entered, and sobbing as if his heart would break, flew to his side.

"Why, Frank!" Percy exclaimed. "What's the matter?"

'I wish I was dead!" sobbed Frank.

This strong expression is common enough in the mouths of passionate children, and also, \'7b am told, of young ladies given to pettishness. But Percy had never before heard so shocking a wish. He was appalled.

"Frank! Frank! don't speak in that way. You surely can't mean such a wicked thing."

"Yes, I can mean it; and I do mean it; and I am wicked. That's just what's the matter/' cried Frank, still sobbing.

"Surely, no one has been teasing you!" "No, they're all nice enough. But they laugh at me."

"I'm sure," said Percy, still stroking the little head —"I'm sure they don't mean any harm. Indeed, the boys who know you like you very much —all of them."

"It doesn't matter—I'm a Jew. I'm sure I am. This morning when we were in that chapel before breakfast, I talked to the fellow next to me; and he wouldn't answer—only grinned. And then when I got upon my seat and looked around, I saw a lot of the boys laughing at me. Oh, I'm sure I'm a Jew!"

Despite his sympathy, Percy was amused. 'What's your idea of a Jew, Frank?"

"I don't know,. But I'll bet it's something bad and ugly and foolish."

"Not at all: Jews may be very excellent people, though they have not the happiness of the true faith. Some of the noblest characters in history were Jews. But as for you—you don't look one bit like a Jew."

"Well, I'm a heathen anyhow," sobbed Frank with lessening grief.

"No indeed, you're not. You're my friend."

Frank did not seem, thus far, to have considered the matter in this light. He ceased sobbing, but his face still gave evidence that he had his doubts.

'Tom Playfair said I was a Jew." 'You don't understand Tom. He was only joking, you know. Tom likes you immensely."

"Does he?" Frank was softening into smiles.

"Yes, indeed! But look, Frank, aren't you coming skating?"

"No, sir," answered Frank, with a relapse into gloom. "I want to stay right here and get religion."

Poor Frank had already become painfully aware of his ignorance in regard to sacred matters; and, being an earnest, ambitious child, it was the consciousness of his inferiority, in this respect, to his college companions which had brought on this burst of feeling, and fortified him to forego the pleasure of a morning on the ice.

"Can't you skate ?" asked Percy, hardly able to suppress a smile at Frank's constant expression, "get religion."

"Oh yes; I know how to skate well enough. And that's why I won't go. You see, I want to learn something I don't know."

"Oh my! Can you skate?" 'Yes; of course."

For the first time in his life, I dare say, Percy indulged in a bit of finesse.

"I'm so glad to hear it," he went on; "because you can do me a great favor."

"Do you a favor?" echoed Frank, his gloom-contracted countenance bursting from apathy into full-blown interest. "Oh, I'm so glad! What is it?"

"Teach me to skate."

Frank's face put on all the wonder it. could assimilate.

"What! what! Don't you know how to skate ?"

"I couldn't make one stroke, Frank; I never had an ice-skate on in my life."

Frank unbent in a radiant smile; then broke \nto a laugh, which he kept up for some time.

'Well, if that isn't funny! And you're ever so much bigger than I am. But I'm so glad I can teach you anything, Percy; and I'm going to teach you to skate, all by myself."

Frank had now brightened up wonderfully. His pessimistic views on the value of life had vanished into thin air; he moved about with alacrity, produced his skates with a certain air of dignity, and breaking into another smile, added:

"I take it all back: I don't wish I was dead. I Want to live and teach you how to skate."

"Thank you, Frank. And can you play baseball?"

"Oh, can't I !" ejaculated Frank with increasing animation.

"Splendid!" said wily Percy. "I can hardly ever hold a ball myself; and I'm very anxious to know how to do it this coming spring."

'Whoop-la!" piped Frank. "I'll teach you myself. Oh, we'll have dead loads of fun!"

This added prospect raised Frank's spirits into the uproarious. He laughed and chatted, and danced about, till Percy declared that he was like a little sunbeam • which remark flattered Frank immensely, and, if possible, made him still more lively.

'I say, Percy Wynn," cried Tom bursting breathlessly into the play-room, "aren't you coming skating?—Why! holloa, old man!"

The "old man" referred to was Frank.

"Yes, Tom," Percy made answer, "I was just about ready to start."

"Good ! I'll give you your first lesson. Aren't you coming too, old man?"

"Yes; and I don't want you to teach Percy, either."

"Depraved youth," said Tom, gravely, "is it thus you wish your friends to be treated? of course I'll teach Percy. And I'll give you all the lessons you want, too, for nothing."

"No, you won't," answered Frank, decidedly. "I know how to skate, and I'm going to teach Percy all alone by myself,"

Frank was jealous.

"Well, old sinner," pursued Tom with a smile, "won't you let me help you?"

Frank made pause, while he considered this question.

"Well," he at length made answer, "you may help, now and then, if you do just what I tell you."

"Thank you, old man; you're a jewel."

The three now set out, and hurrying forward, fell behind the foremost boys who were advancing at a smart pace towards the river.

"Tom," began Frank when the trio had swung themselves into a steady pace, "what's a sinner? YOU called me a sinner just now."

"Yes, but I was joking," answered Tom, who was beginning to perceive that his little friend was apt to take remarks very literally. "A sinner is a person who does very bad things. Of course you're not a sinner."

Frank pondered for a moment; then went on:

"Is a boy who hates people, and who wishes he was dead, a sinner?"

"I guess he is, if he hates them very much, and really wishes he was dead."

'Then I'm a sinner," calmly added the logical youth of ten summers, "and you were right when you called me one. But I'm going to get over it. I'm going to change. I'm going to get religion."

"You talk about getting religion as if it were put up in packages," said Tom, smiling.

"Yes," assented Percy. "But that's the way some people not of our faith talk. I've often seen it in books. They don't reform or become good; they always 'get religion.'

As they pursued their way, Percy and Tom were kept very busy answering Frank's questions. Prayer, Mass, and a hundred other sacred matters were touched upon; and Frank was thoroughly pleased with the information he received concerning these things. Truly, after a life-long abstinence, his soul had become hungry. And when Percy, in sweet and gracious manner, told him the leading events in the his* tory of our divine Lord, the child's intelligent face glowed with sympathetic interest.

"Are you sure that He loved little children very much?" asked Frank.

"Certain," Percy made answer. "He spoke of them so often and so lovingly. Once, when His disciples wished to keep them away from Him, He gave them a scolding, and said that in heaven all were like little children."

'Well," said Frank, with much seriousness, "I'm going to love Him back, since He loved me. And I'm going to write to my papa, and tell him the whole story; and papa will love Him too."

They were now at the river's bank.

When it came to putting on their skates, Frank was quite indignant at Tom's undertaking to assist Percy.

"No, you don't!" he exclaimed, with no little warmth. "You just go and put on your own skates. I'll attend to Percy myself."

Tom laughingly obeyed; and Frank, with a sense of importance which he made no attempt to conceal, took Percy under his own special and sole charge. When all was ready for the start, he caught Percy's hand.

"Here, Tom—Tom Playfair," he then called out, "you may take Percy's left hand; but mind you're very careful not to go too fast."

"Holloa!" cried John Donnel, dashing at full tilt into the party, and neatly stopping himself by running squarely into Tom. "I thought, Percy, I was under contract to teach you how to skate."

"Go away, John Donnel!" commanded Frank. "I won't allow it. Clear off, now. He's in my charge"

So delighted and so impressed was Frank with his assumed task that he would hardly allow any one to approach Percy at all. For all that, however, he was a skilful skater, and with such earnestness did he coach Percy that our hero was soon initiated into the mystery of "striking out."

"Hurrah!" cried Frank, when this important point had been gained, "ain't I a good teacher !"

"Splen —did," answered Percy as he struck out anew, and sat down very suddenly on the ice.

"Are you hurt?" cried Frank, with real concern.

"Oh dear! no; but how shall I get up?" 'Torn Playfair—do you hear me?" (Tom was trying his foot on the Dutch Roll hard by.) 'Tom, come on here and help."

"First class, Percy," Tom remarked as he assisted Frank to bring the beginner to his feet. "Every skater must learn to cut a star, and you've got that down fine already."

'Where's the star, Tom?" Percy asked.

"It's gone now; but you cut it all the same."

"See here, Tom Playfair," put in Frank, who took life quite seriously, "I don't want you to make fun of Percy's skating."

"Oh, I beg your pardon, Professor Burdock; but honestly you are teaching him very well."

Mollified by this compliment, the professor continued his lesson. Within an hour, Percy, who was blessed with strong ankles, found himself able to stand on his legs without help; and before a second hour had elapsed, he was able to move about unassisted. And yet the awkward figure which the naturally graceful boy presented on the ice was ridiculous to see; and I am afraid that Frank made some very rash offers to punch the head of a few boys double his size because they dared laugh at his pupil. He was quite enthusiastic about the success of his new friend, and on the road homewards offered to bet Harry Quip any sum of money under a million dollars that before the end of the win-

ter, Percy would be the most accomplished skater in the small yard.

On arriving at the college, Frank called Mr. Middleton aside, and with an air of mystery began :

'You mustn't tell any one what I'm going to say to you, Mr. Middleton."

"Very well, Frank."

"What I want to know, is—can you prove there's a God?"

'Yes, I believe I can."

"Will you please prove it?"

Mr. Middleton, suiting his expressions, as far as could be, to the age of the precocious sceptic, explained several of the most evident arguments in favor of the existence of a Supreme Being. With close attention, the child listened to the clear exposition.

"I see it, now, Mr. Middleton," he said, when the prefect had come to a pause. "But do you know, it seems so queer. I don't feel as if I were the same boy at all that I was two days ago. Everything looks so different. Percy told me that there was a God, but he didn't prove it. I want things proved. I'm so glad to know it's true. Mr. Middleton, I want to ask you something else. Is it bad to hate people?' 1

"Of course. God loves all men, and He wants us to love them, too."

"Well, Mr. Middleton, would you think a boy like me, and my size, could be bad, and even wish he was dead?"

"Why not? Little boys can be wicked, as well as grown men. St. Augustine, who lived a very holy life when he had become a grown

man, said of his boyhood, 'Tantillus puer et tantus peccator' —'So small a boy, so great a sinner.' He was a bad boy; but got over it."

"I'm glad to know that. I was thinking, you see, that I wasn't like anybody else. I've been horrid"

Mr. Middleton laughed at this naive con-fession.

"Oh; but I'm bad—terribly bad," protested Frank. "I'd like to shoot Buck; and this morning I got mad and wished I was dead."

"But now that you know it's very wrong, would you shoot Buck if you had the chance?"

"No — o! I wouldn't now; but I'd like to."

"Then it's not so wrong."

To Frank's evident relief, Mr. Middleton explained that wickedness does not consist in the way we feel, but in the yielding to our bad feelings. He showed that the inclination to do wrong is a temptation —not in itself a sin, but capable of becoming sinful by the assent of the free will. All of this he made clear by an abundance of practical examples.

"Thank you, sir," said Frank, when he had mastered the explanation. "I'm going to be good after this. Will you help me?"

"Certainly, my dear boy; and to-morrow when we commemorate the birth of the Infant Jesus, ask Him to help you, too."

"Indeed I will, sir. He loved little boys, so Percy told me, and I love Him; and I'm going to try to do something to please Him. And I'm going to write to my papa and get him to love Our Lord, too."

Christmas morning dawned, ushered in by a

snowstorm. According to the sweet and hallowed custom of the place, the students attended three Masses. The clear voices of the singers — faint echoes of the angelic choirs; the beautiful vestments of celebrant and acolytes; the joyous decorations and splendor of the altar; above all, the fervor and devotion, which cast gleams of glory over the faces of the young worshippers, filled Frank with wonder and delight. But hardly did he take his eyes for a moment from the pretty Bethlehem crib. Quite naturally he joined his little hands in prayer for the first time, and begged the sweet Infant Who so loved little children to enrich him with feelings of kindness and good-will towards all his fellow creatures.

As the students, at the end of the ceremonies, were descending the stairs to the refectory, Percy, catching up with Frank, clapped him on the back.

"Happy Christmas, Frank!"

"Oh, it is happy! I never felt so happy in all my life. Percy, your religion is mine. It's all so nice. Say: let's stop here on the stairs a moment. I want to catch Donnel and Keenan, and Harry and Tom."

Percy called these as they were passing.

Schoolboy-like, and Christmas-like, they were all happy and smiling, shaking hands with each other heartily, and speaking from full hearts those pretty words, so fitting to the time, so sweetened by precious memories.

"Boys," said Frank, earnestly, when he had at length secured their attention, "I've been praying at the Infant Jesus; and I want to join

your religion. I'll never wish I was dead again; and if Buck were drowning in the river," concluded the little rmte, impressively, s Td jump right in and save him!"

CHAPTER XXII A Merry Christmas to All

TT WAS a joyful Hreakfast tfiat Christmas morning. Loud were the exclamations of pleasure and pleased surprise, as each boy, on lifting his plate, found beneath it a pretty Christmas-card.

"It never happened before," remarked Harry Quip, who had been attending St. Maure's for three years. "Mr. Middleton is always getting up some nice surprise. He's a trump!"

"It makes the place so like home," Joe Whyte observed.

"But isn't it a glorious Christmas morning?" exclaimed Willie Ruthers. "The snow is falling so nicely. A Christmas without snow is like a story without an end."

"Or bread without butter," put in Joe.

"Or an angel without wings," added Donnel* who presided over this cheerful table.

"Or a cat without its meow!" chuckled Harry.

All the other tables were accommodating an equally jolly company. Loud praises of Mr. Middleton, merry greetings, jokes and jests flew from mouth to mouth; while above the din could be heard the musical voice of Percy, and the shrill, piercing laugh of Frankie Burdock, for the nonce the lightest heart of all. It was indeed a merry Christmas.

Breakfast ended, Mr. Middleton announced that the Christmas-boxes from home were all awaiting the inspection of their owners in the study-hall. Then reading out the names of those whose boxes had arrived—with the exception of Frank and a very few others, all were on the list —he requested the happy proprietors not to eat any of the good things till the regular hour set apart for this purpose—ten o'clock of the forenoon. This visit extraordinary, he explained, was simply allowed for the purpose of gratifying a natural and legitimate curiosity.

Forthwith there was a tremendous hurrying, pushing, and crowding, each boy striving to be the first out of the refectory. The exodus, it must be confessed, was rather disorderly. Mr. Middleton remained calm, however. "Christmas," he reflected, "comes but once a year."

When Frank had succeeded in making his way through the crush at the refectory door, he found Percy, Tom, and Harry awaiting him.

"Come on, old man!" cried Tom; "we want you to help us look at our boxes."

'There's none for me," Frank made answer in a sad tone. "My papa doesn't believe in Christmas yet. He'll never think of sending me a Christmas-box. But he's just as kind as can be. No; I don't care about going up."

"Frank, do come," pleaded Percy in his most persuasive accents. "Half the pleasure of opening my box will be gone if you don't come along."

"Same way with me," said Tom.

"Me, too," added Harry.

"Then, I'll go," said Frank.

They ascended the study-hall stairs. The large room presented a very cheerful appearance indeed. The study-benches had been removed the day previous. On the floor, alongside the wall, were disposed very small boxes and very big boxes and boxes of all sizes between; their owners* names, to avoid mistakes, clearly written on slips of paper pinned upon the wainscot. The boys were in great excitement. Some were tripping hither and thither, looking for their names; others, down on their knees before their discovered property, were feverishly pulling out every conceivable form of present from the Christmas turkey to the Christmas illustrated magazine; others, again, were dancing about their boxes, pleasantly tantalizing themselves as to what were the hidden treasures within: everybody was talking either to his neighbor or, if his neighbor chanced to be over-occupied, to himself. On this occasion, the walls may have had ears; certainly the boys had not.

Percy, with Frank at his side, soon found his box: no difficult matter after all, for it was an enormous box—the largest in the room.

"Oh my! what a big box!" Frank observed.

"Well, you see I've got ten sisters," explained Percy, merrily, as he stopped and threw back the cover, "and every one of them has to put in her particular gift. They're nice girls: they're so fond of me."

The box proved to be a veritable curiosity-shop: books in pretty holiday binding, magazines with colored engravings, exquisite Christmas-cards, gloves, shoes, a sealskin cap, ear-muff, silk scarfs, neck-ties, boxes of fine French candy, the traditional turkey, cakes, fruit, nuts — my pen in putting them down is getting weary.

As these gifts emerged from their obscurity, Frank's eyes opened very wide; he was as fully delighted that they were for Percy as though they were all for himself, and, momentarily throwing off his old-fashioned ways, he broke into cheers and danced about the box.

"Look, Frank, look! I knew there was something for you," said Percy, taking up the prettiest of the silken scarfs, and attempting to put it around Frank's neck. But the lad drew back.

"No, no," he piped, "it's yours; everything's yours."

"But this is for you, Frank."

"Prove it! prove it!" cried the infant logician.

"If you don't take this scarf," said Percy, ceasing to smile, "I'll not enjoy my box near so much. See! there's a whole lot of scarfs; I don't want them all."

Frank suffered himself to be persuaded; and Percy in his dainty way adjusted the gift about his little friend's neck in the most approved taste. Notwithstanding his refusal at first, Frank was very proud of his present, and could not conceal his happiness. His bright chestnut eyes sparkled with pleasure, as he tripped across the room to show Tom his acquisition.

'Why, old man, what's this? You're a regular out-and-out dude."

"Don't care a snap what I am. It's from Percy."

"But what's the matter with your jacket-pockets ?" asked Tom, gravely. "They look queer."

"What is it, Tom? Are they torn?"

"Come here: I'll show you."

Frank drew nearer, and Tom, catching him in a firm hold, proceeded to fill his pockets with candy, nuts, and raisins.

"Now they look all right— as sound and as large as the moon when it's full."

"Come back here, Frank," interrupted Percy, "I want you."

Frank, in great glee, skipped across to Percy.

"Here's something else for you, Frank. Oh, you needn"t draw back. It's a prayer-book, and I have three already. You'll need one, you know, if you want to 'get religion/

Frank was too delighted for words. He took the beautiful silver-clasped book of devotion, opened it with eagerness, and ran over page after page. Presently a picture fell out.

"Oh! Oh! Look!" he exclaimed, picking it up. "If it isn't the Stable at Bethlehem, and the Little Babe Who loved children! Isn't it nice! Here, Percy, you take it; it's yours."

"No, indeed," Percy made answer, "it's for you. Everything in the book is for you. It's my Christmas gift for little Frank."

'I'll be big some day," answered Frank, seriously, "and then I intend to give you a house and lot with a carriage, and a coachman in ? cocked hat and gold buttons on his coat."

"And what'll you give Tom?" asked Percy t struggling to keep a straight face.

"I'll give him a bag of gold."

Frank was precocious ; but in many things h* was far from being an "old man."

Word went round among the boys that "little Frank," as they called him, had not received a Christmas-box. This was enough to awaken their sympathies. Donnel, Keenan, Richards, and indeed a host of the students, were soon upon him with every imaginable species of confectionery. Frank had his breath fairly taken away by their kindness. That his papa should shower attentions upon him was a matter which he had been brought up to expect. But that these boys, comparative strangers to him, should be lavish of kind words and gifts was something he could scarcely realize. In sheer self-protection from their exuberance of kindness, he made his escape from the study-hall.

For the first time since his arrival in St. Maure's, Percy plotted a practical joke. Calling together Tom, Donnel, Keenan, Quip, and a few others, he thus spoke:

"Boys, I've an idea."

"Hurrah!" said Tom, ironically. "Hear! hear!"

"Poor Frank's father will hardly think of sending him a Christmas-box. Suppose we club together and get up one for him ourselves. He won't think we did it, if we go about it quietly. It'll be a good joke."

"Oh, it's just too funny!" said Harry, solemnly. "But, joke or not, it's just the thing. I've got something that will suit Frank to a dot. My grandma's got the idea that I'm no older now than when I last saw her. I was seven then."

"Your grandma is perfectly right," muttered Tom in parenthesis.

"Well, anyhow, she's sent me an immense picture-book with all kinds of fairy tales told in words of not more than two syllables. It's the very thing for Frank."

"That is," interposed Keenan, "if you're willing to give it up. It's just what you need, you know. For my part, I'll undertake to supply a box of candy. '

"And I," said Donnel, "a turkey. But I won't starve, all the same. I'll live on your turkey, George."

Before the boys had finished declaring what they should give of their abundance, Tom, who had left them for a moment, entered with a large box. Forthwith, in went candy, oranges, cakes, turkey, books, and what not. In a short time, there awaited Frank a box in no wise inferior to the best in the hall.

And so, when ten o'clock had come, Frank was informed by Mr. Kane, who enjoyed the confidence of the conspirators, that something had arrived for him, too. Frank dashed off to the study-hall; and it was indeed ludicrous, a moment later, to see him running about among his friends, and insisting on their taking a share of the good things. In some cases, the generous lads were fairly forced by the ardent Frank to receive what they themselves had given.

The day, it is almost needless to remark, passed very happily; and at night a climax of enjoyment was reached when Dickens' famour Christmas Carol of Scrooge & Marley (drama< tized by one of the professors) was played before faculty and students.

In the opening scene, Frank, who had had no previous theatrical experience, created quite a diversion. He had been listening for some time, with ill-concealed indignation, to Scrooge's remarks; but when that hard-handed griping, business-machine said with great disdain: "Christmas!—Humbug!" Frank could restrain himself no longer.

Mounting his chair, he stamped his foot, and angrily shook his diminutive fist at the brutal miser.

"It's a lie, you old Scrooge! And you ought to be ashamed of yourself. You're a wicked—
"

The rest of the sentence was cut short by the energetic action of Tom, who, catching the indignant orator's feet, brought him down rather suddenly.

Amidst the roar that greeted this diversion, Tom and Percy explained to Frank the nature and objects of plays in general; which so cleared that young gentleman's mind that he presently expressed himself satisfied, and implied that he had no objections to the performances going on.

In the dormitory that night, Frank, before retiring to rest, knelt down after the manner of his friends, and, placing before him the picture of the Nativity, clasped his hands in prayer. An hour later, Mr. Middleton, noticing that the child manifested no disposition to retire, thought it well to put an end to these lengthy devotions. On advancing to Frank's side, however, he found that the kneeling lad,

worn out with the pleasures and emotions of the day, was peacefully sleeping, his lips pressed upon the picture of the "Infant Who loved little children."

An Adventure on the Railroad-Track

TT WOULD be a long task to describe in detail

the varied amusements of Christmas week. Skating, dancing, the nightly play, in-door games and out-door sport, caused these days to pass on the wings of happiness and mirth.

With all this, little Frank contrived to "get religion" in time and out of time. Just six days after his arrival, he was reduced to tears, and, I regret to state, made quite a show of temper, when his peremptory request that the president should baptize him on the spot was denied. But he soon regained his calmness of demeanor, and, under favor of the president's promise that he should be baptized, once he knew his catechism well by heart, he set to work at the study of this little book with such ardor that Percy could scarcely persuade him to come out skating.

Frank very effectually prevented Mr. Kane and Mr. Middleton from becoming lonesome. No sooner did either of these worthy prefects put in an appearance in the yard than he bore down upon him and played the part of an animated interrogation-point. Like the gentlemen of the court-room, Frank wanted "the truth, the whole truth, and nothing but the truth."

He was especially hard upon Mr. Middle-ton.

230

"Prove it!" he would calmly say when Mr, Middleton had advanced some simple statement which any other boy living would have taken for granted.

But beyond all doubt, he did master his catechism. Only as a matter of prudence was his reception into the Church delayed. Meanwhile Percy picked up so rapidly in skating that his professor could gracefully allow his pupil to shift for himself. Percy was still awkward upon the ice; but that defect, like youthfulness, is something which time alone ?an correct.

On the last day of the old year, an event occurred which exercised a strong influence upon Percy's character.

Shortly after breakfast, the boys went to "the lakes" for a day's skating. Early in the afternoon, Percy, feeling unwell, obtained permission from the presiding prefect to return to college. Frank wished to serve as his companion, but Percy would not hear of this.

"No, you stay, Frank. You need a little more out-door exercise. You're wearing your little brains out with that catechism. I think Tom had better come with me."

This choice of Tom had, most probably, an important bearing on after-events. They walked along the railroad track for over a mile without meeting with any one. But just as they were about to pass over a trestle-work bridge (intended only for engine and cars) above a deep ravine, a man, who had been hidden from their sight by the steep bank, arose and, taking his station on the track,

awaited their advance. He was gaunt, and haggard of face. His beard, of several days* growth, imparted to his features a weird aspect. His eyes, deep-sunk, glittered with a dreadful light. The clothes upon him were tattered, scanty — too few, God knows, for such bitter weather. His shoes scarcely pro-tected his feet at all. Standing there on the railroad-track, with his pinched features, shining eyes, and wretched attire, he was the picture of misery and woe.

"Oh, Tom," Percy exclaimed in a whisper, as he caught Tom's arm, "let's turn back; that man looks like a wolf. He's a stick in his hand, too. Perhaps he may attack us."

"Oh, I guess not," said Tom, coolly. "But if he starts to attack, it will be time enough to run away then."

So Tom, with Percy timidly clinging to his arm, walked boldly on.

"Good-evening," he said, as they arrived within a few feet of the wretch who was evidently awaiting them.

The man scanned them hungrily; then fastened his eyes on Percy. Percy shivered.

"Boy," he said, "what time is it?"

Percy with trembling fingers took out his watch.

"Half-past two, sir."

The man advanced a step on them. Tom drew Percy back.

"Keep off, will you?" Tom exclaimed. "I reckon you're near enough."

Upon seeing Percy's handsome gold watch,

the man's features had, if possible, taken on a yet hungrier appearance.

"Hand me that watch, young fellow, and I'll let you both go."

'We've got to run," whispered Tom quickly; and he and Percy, both thoroughly frightened turned and dashed back towards the lakes. At once the man was after them, and the sound of his footfalls at their back inspired both boys to tremendous exertions.

"Quicker —quicker yet!" panted Tom as they sped on, not even daring to look around at their pursuer, lest they should lose ground. "I think he's gaining on us."

They made forward for some time in si-fence, not a sound upon the stillness save their own labored breathing and the ominous footfall behind.

Presently Tom, judging from the sound of the pursuer's feet that it would be safe, ventured to turn his head.

"Cheer up, Percy," he said. "He's falling back. At first I think he gained on us, but now he's losing awfully."

A minute passed.

Tom took another look.

"He's almost out of the race. He can't run worth a cent."

Presently he added:

'Why, he has stopped. Hold on; we're all right, Percy. He's at least two hundred feet off. Let's take a rest, too."

Both turned, and, feeling that they were out of danger, took a full look at their defeated pursuer. An exclamation of surprise

broke from the lips of Percy. The man's actions were certainly strange. Not only had he stopped; he had taken a seat on a railroad-tie

"'Well, I declare!'/ said Tom. "He doesn't take much interest in gold watches after all. Halloa!"

This explanation was evoked by the man's lying down across the track.

"Oh, my God!" cried Percy in dismay.

"Is he out of his mind?" queried Tom.

"No," answered Percy. "I am beginning to see now. That man must be sick. Do ou remember the look of his thin face, and is hollow eye? Tom, we must go to him."

Percy was now as resolute as he had before been timid.

"All right," Tom agreed. "But to make sure, I'll get something to protect ourselves with."

He quickly secured a stout stick, which he happened to perceive lying near by, and armed with this, he and Percy advanced towards their pursuer.

"Say," exclaimed Tom, when they had come within a few yards of the motionless form, "get up off the track. There may be a train along here any minute."

At these words, the man raised his head and stared at them listlessly.

"Are you sick?" pursued Tom.

"I'm dying."

There was a dread solemnity about those two words which, were Percy and Tom to live into the centuries, they will never forget.

"Oh, my God!" cried Percy, clasping his hands.

Tom's tone and feelings were at once changed.

"Can we help you, my poor fellow?" he asked; and throwing aside his stick, he advanced with Percy.

The man paused, then answered slowly:

"I'm past help, I think."

Percy had been gazing at him intently.

"Oh, Tom, Tom! he's starving!" And Percy sobbed.

The man looked up with a bewildered air.

"I am starving, boy," he said.

Tom happened to have a cake in his pocket. He drew it forth and handed it to the poor creature.

"Try to eat it," he said gently and tenderly. "It's the only thing I've got, my friend."

The man accepted the gift, and made an attempt to eat. In the very act, a sudden fit of coughing came upon him, and he spat out a mouthful of blood.

"Thank you, my boy, 11 he said feebly. "I'm past the need of bread."

"Shall we take you off the track, sir?" asked Tom.

The poor fellow, who had raised himself upon his skinny arm to receive the cake, in lieu of answer to this question fell back helplessly.

Tom, throwing off his overcoat and jacket, spread them on a patch of soft earth just beside the railroad-track.

"We must catch hold of him, and place him there, Percy/' he said gravely.

They carried the poor fellow with little trouble—he was light enough—to this spot. Then Percy drew off his coat and wrapped it around their patient.

Tom would have restrained him.

"You're sick yourself, Percy," he said; "you'll risk injuring yourself." 'This is a time for risks, Tom."

The man's fierce aspect had softened.

"You're good boys—good boys," he panted. "I'm sorry. I should have asked you for help, instead of trying to rob you."

There was a moment's pause. Tom was in a brown study. Save the labored breathing of the dying wretch, there was a deathly stillness.

"Percy," said Tom at length, "are you afraid to stay alone with this poor man?"

"Oh no."

"I think he is dying. And it seems to me one of us should go for assistance."

'Til stay, Tom. You are the better runner."

"Very well. I'll run to St. Maure's and try to get a wagon or something."

And Tom, at his highest speed, started across the trestle-work bridge, heedless of the danger. Danger! was there not a life in question?

So there stood Percy alone with the sick man.

"Cheer up, sir," he said presently. "Tom has run on to get assistance."

"It's too late."

"Do you really think you're going to die?"

"Yes."

Percy breathed a prayer to the Blessed Vir* gin.

Then he again spoke.

"Well, if you're going to die, sir, hadn't you better think of the other world?"

The man's face, thus far apathetic, became troubled.

"I'm going to hell," he said. "For the last two years I've been leading a very wicked life.'*

Percy dwelt upon these words.

"But you weren't always wicked?" he at length said.

"No d , once I was happy and contented. Then I wasn't so bad." As he spoke, fresh life seemed to infuse itself into the man. "I was happy in a dear wife and an only child— a boy." Here the narrator raised himself on his arm, and continued with more animation. "I was what they call a 'skilled mechanic/ and received very good wages. But troubles came on between some of the men and the bosses. There was a strike. I was a member of an association, and had to go out with the rest. The strike passed away; but my work never came back. I saw my wife's cheeks grow paler day by day. I saw her face grow thinner and thinner. Then I offered myself for any kind of work. But even with the poor work and poor pay I got, it was too late. When she smiled upon me for the last time, and died of want, I gave up God."

"Oh> poor fellow!" Percy exclaimed, the tears arising to his eyes. "It was hard; but you should have prayed the more. Here—it is hard for you to rest on your hand; put your head on my knees."

Percy seated himself, and placed the man in this easier position.

'You are a good boy. I would like to say 4 God bless you;' but it would mean nothing from me. As I was saying, my boy was left me —and how I loved him; and worked, worked, worked at anything to provide for him. But the times grew worse; he died of fever. Then I cursed God."

A visible shudder passed over Pр and while he said nothing aloud, his lips moved in prayer.

"I was almost crazed with grief/* continued the man. "From that hour I hated the wealthy; I hated law, I hated order It was wrong, I knew; but I was determined to live wicked. From that hour I became a tramp, a thief, a companion of villains and murderers. And now you ask me to think of another life? I have no hope."

"But God will forgive you if you repent."

The man considered. Percy, whose whole soul was bent in bringing his companion to repentance, noticed, even as he watched the haggard countenance, that snow was beginning to fall, silent and soft.

U I cannot hope it; no, I've lived bad, and I'll die bad."

"But think of Jesus dying on the cross," urged Percy, his face kindling with earnestness. "He shed every drop of His blood for you."

'Yes," came the groaning answer, "and I've spurned it."

In the agitation of the moment, Percy prayed aloud.

"O my God, my God! what shall I say to bring this creature to Thee? — My friend, my dear friend, on that cross, and while He was suffering so bitterly, Christ forgave a thief who had been leading a whole life of sin. Now Christ is no longer in bitter pain; He is happy. Speak to Him, my friend. You have sinned, but He will forgive you. It is impossible for you to go to confession, but do make your peace with God. You have but one soul."

The man listened earnestly. With each sec* ond the pallor upon his face was increasing; and now drops of sweat were standing upon his brow. Even at this supreme moment, when the judgment-seat of God seemed to be awaiting an immortal soul, Percy observed that the flakes were falling faster each minute.

"D© you think He might forgive me?"

"Oh, surely! And I think He will pity and love you the more, my friend, for the very reason that you are dying like Him — under the sky, and deserted by all."

"Oh, if I could repent! I fear it is too late."

More slowly, more heavily, he was fetching his breath. The snow was falling thicker and faster. Percy realized with a sense of awe, such as he had never felt before, that a soul was, as it were, in his keeping. Suddenly his face lighted up as with an inspiration. He placed his hand in his pocket, and drew forth a small silver crucifix— a Christmas present from one of his sisters.

"Kiss it, my friend, for the love and the memory of Our Saviour, Who died on the cross."

"I'm afraid to dare it," moaned the wretch with a shiver. "Oh, God! I have been so wicked. I am corrupt. Go away from me, boy I I am not even worthy to be near a pure child. I am cursed. Leave me."

In answer to this, Percy raised the dying creature's pallid head and imprinted a kiss on the forehead. "O my God," he murmured in the act, "have pity on him."

The dying man's face softened still more.

"My boy," he said, "if you are so good, God must be good, too."

"Yes, yes," said Percy, eagerly; "He is infinitely good."

Every word, every breath on the part of the dying man was now an effort. About that poor creature, struggling for air and life, frolicked the madcap snow.

"But—He—knows"—he paused for a time, through sheer lack of strength, then went on— "all my sins; you don't."

"As God is looking down on us, my friend, I know that He will forgive you and love you, even were your sins a thousand times greater than they are."

A moment's silence, broken by the long-drawn gasps of the dying. He made an attempt to speak. Percy bent nearer to catch the words.

"Crucifix!"—that was what the boy made out. Percy brought the crucifix to the man's lips. He kissed it tenderly.

'Thank God!" murmured Percy. He added aloud: "Now, my dear friend, if you wish to enjoy the company of Jesus forever; if you wish to see your wife and little boy again, you

must make an act of perfect contrition for your sins. Do you wish to do so?"

The man nodded his head in assent.

'Well: it is a great grace. You must be sorry for having offended God, Who is infinitely perfect and good. Now pray to God quietly and from your heart for one moment that you may get this grace. I shall pray with you."

There was a period of silence. In the palpable stillness, the snow was falling more and more quickly. Again the awful silence was broken by the whistle of a train far up the track.

"Come," resumed Percy, as the faint echo of the whistle died away; "are you ready?"

The upturned face signified assent.

"Good. Now repeat the words after me as I speak them. And first of all, kiss the crucifix once more.'

As the man complied, the rumble of a distant train came faintly on their ears.

"Now," continued Percy, "repeat after me: 'My Jesus, mercy.'

Percy bent low to catch the faintest whisper; the rumbling noise was growing more distinct. Percy had read of the death-rattle. Even as he bent over, he heard an ominous sound from the man's throat. Surely there could be no time to lose.

"Oh, my God," he said.

"Oh, my God," repeated the dying man. 'I am most heartily sorry" —

The rumble was now sharpening into a rattle.

"For all my sins."

"And I detest them" —

"From the bottom of my heart."

As Percy stooped to catch these last words, the man broke into a cough; more blood came; and while the train in its magnificence swept by, bearing with it strength and power and wealth, bearing with it mortals whose fattened purses had never opened to aid poverty, to aid distress, bearing with it a multitude sufficient, in united action, to save a million from death and despair —this outcast of the world, this wretched sport of seeming caprice, went forth in prayer to meet his God.

Let men call him socialist, anarchist, a creature worthy of the halter. Yes, let us punish our anarchists when they violate our most sacred' laws. But we shall save prison fare, and more, if we treat the poor and the oppressed as true children of the One Father, Who is in heaven.

In which Tom Meets Two Young Gentlemen Whom He is not at all Anxious to See

\/f EANTIME Tom was on his way village-ward. For fully a mile his sturdy little legs bore him bravely along. The weather was cold, the air keen; Tom was strong as to chest and limbs; the exercise, to one of his endurance, was refreshing. His breath came and went with the steadiness and fullness of a professional sprint-runner. With his hat well down over his eyes, head erect, chest inflated, his elbows pressed tightly to his side, his fists doubled, he formed a pleasant picture to all lovers of athletics. None were there, indeed, as he sped onwards at a sturdy, unfaltering pace.

Very soon he came in sight of the village.

"Brace up, old fellow!" he whispered to himself. "Come on, now, for all you're worth. It's a good mile off yet, but you must make it under eight minutes or you're no good."

"Yes," he added presently, "I'll be there in six minutes, sure."

But there's many a slip. Hardly had he finished addressing himself the remark just set down, when he perceived in the distance two figures advancing along the railroad-track. They were both human beings and of the mas-

243

culine gender; that he could make out. But whether they were men or boys, his eyesight failed to reveal.

'Wonder who they are!" he muttered. "Well, I hope they're friends in need. Anyhow, I'll know soon, as they're walking towards

me.'

Presently he described a small wicker basket dependent on an arm of one, and three or four skates linked together by a strap in the hands of the other. The bearer of the skates was much the smaller of the two, and clearly a boy.

As Tom drew within the range of accurate eyeshot, he gave a low, prolonged whistle. Both were boys, and boys, too, that he desired to sec least of all the boys dwelling at that moment upon the round earth. The larger he easily recognized as Donnel's village gladiator—the famous Buck; the smaller lad, as Tom rightly inferred, was George Keenan's whilom opponent.

They, in turn, seemed to recognize Tom as a pupil of St. Maure's College (the village youth had an unerring instinct when it came to making out a college-boy), for they at once so altered their proceedings as to give a strong and unequivocal hint of coming trouble. The smaller hero—Buck's young satellite — at once threw down his skates beside the railroad track, and r unmindful of the sharp weather, proceeded to pull off his coat in such wise as to leave no doubt in Tom's mind concerning the smaller hero's intentions; while the adolescent Buck carefully deposited his basket on the bare earth, and com-

posed his rugged features into a malignant scowl.

"Here's a how-d'ye-do !" muttered Tom to himself. "I'm in for it now and no mistake. I'd give two cents for a base-ball bat. And, besides, I'm in no humor for fussing just now, anyhow."

He stopped running a few yards in front of the two belligerents, and was taking a few slow breaths of air preparatory to speaking, when Buck saved him that office by opening the conversation himself.

"See here, you mean little college-chap," began the gloomy-browed Buck with fierce earnestness, "we're looking for fellows like you."

"Come on, you college dandy, and fight!" vociferated Buck's young friend, in a tone of far less dignity, but of equal earnestness. He had already rolled back his shirt-sleeves to the elbow, revealing two very well-developed forearms; and, as he spoke, was executing a novel and ludicrous war-dance, consisting mainly of a hop forward, a hop backward, and a wild brandishing of fists; with an occasional leap into the air by way of interlude. In the midst of these sprightly movements, he took occasion to dash his ragged hat upon the ground with a high disdain of all damages to that valuable bit of wearing apparel.

Buck, putting his arms akimbo, watched these terpsichorean proceedings with gloomy approval.

The dancer continued his speech:

"I can lick any boy my size in that dude School. Come on, will you? I'll black your

eyes for you, I'll bloody your nose, and I'll warm your ears. Come on, won't you? Come on, I say."

As Tom, standing stock still in front of his new acquaintances, listened to this strain of rough, hearty, unscholared eloquence, and gazed upon its dancing author, he forgot, for a moment, his sacred mission. A merry twinkle shot from his eyes, and the muscles of his face so twitched that he could hardly refrain, to use his own subsequent expression, from "letting his smiles loose." The twinkle of the eye escaped the attention of the pugnacious orator; but he observed the facial twitching, and inferred, rashly enough, that Tom was frightened. Hereupon he became more eloquent; there was even a touch of pathos in his tones.

"Come on, you bantam!" he implored. "Come on, you blow-hard! I'll fight fair, and just paralyze you. Come on, now. Come on, will you?" Here his dance became more impassioned. "I'll whip you so's your own mother won't know you."

But all these allurements only served to introduce new twitches into Tom's face, and to intensify those already there. Suddenly, however, he sobered. The snow had just begun to fall, and the memory of Percy and the dying man—both exposed to the inclemency of the season— shot back through his mind in all its vividness.

"See here, boys," he said in all seriousness, "I'm in no humor for fighting just now. There's a man down—"

"None of your lies," broke in Buck. "We

don't care whether you feel like fighting or not. But if you don't go to work, and fight Dick like a man, I'll thrash you till you'll wish you were in Chiny."

During this speech of the great leader, Dick was still "leading the dance," and, in a steady flow of cordial eloquence, adjuring Tom to

"come on."

But Tom was clinging earnestly to the memory of the dying scene he had left at his back.

"I won't fight," he said decisively.

"You won't!" exclaimed Buck. "I knew you was a coward. Go for him, Dick! Make him fight, anyhow."

At the word of command, Dick advanced, and made a savage drive at Tom, who at once put up his hands. The blow was but partially warded off, however. Its force was diminished; yet, for all that, it brought out an ugly mark on Tom's cheek.

Tom was by no means an over-passionate boy, nor, on the other hand, was he an angel in temper. We find that even the meekest of mortals fly into a passion on being struck. Tom was not the meekest of mortals. He flushed angrily — for the second time the memory of his mission was driven out of his head — doubled his fists and flashed back a blow at his assailant. The blow was well directed. It struck Dick squarely on the face, and sent him staggering backwards. Tom might have followed up his advantage with ease, and indeed was on the point of doing so when suddenly his memory asserted itself. There again he saw the dying man, the exposed child, the soul—the

precious, immortal soul—in the balance. He breathed a prayer for courage. Grace came down upon him, soft and radiant as the gentle snow-flakes now thickening the air. He threw down his hands.

"Come on," he said, "both of you: you can go ahead and beat me till you're tired. I ask you only one favor. There's a man—a poor starving man—dying, up the track. When you're through with me, for God's sake go to his help! I'm not going to fight with a man's life on my hands. And, Dick, I ask your pardon, honestly, for striking you."

During these words, one of Tom's hands had gone into his jacket. Doubtless it was clasping that old, old scapular of the Sacred Heart which he had once shown to Percy. He was thus seeking help to bear manfully the savage revenge of these two boys. His cheeks had blanched; but his eye was steady.

However, he was not called upon for a great trial of endurance. His words must have been the echoes of whispered voices of grace, for no speech could have had a more impressive ef~-fect.

Dick blushed —actually blushed. He appeared to be thoroughly ashamed of himself, and hastily began to pull down his sleeves. Buck's face relaxed from its gloomy sternness; it softened visibly, and became almost tender in its expression.

U A poor man dying of starvation!" he exclaimed. 'Why didn't you say so before ? We wouldn't have hindered you none if we'd know» that. If it'll be any help to you, I've got a bot-tie of wine with me in that basket. It ain't much, I know; but you're welcome to it."

"You have !" cried Tom with animation. "Just the thing! It may save him. But there's no time to lose; we've got to hurry up. He's not much more than a mile off."

"Come on, then," said Buck, catching up the basket. 'We'll get there on a run."

"Say," put in Dick, hurriedly, "can't I be of any help?"

These words were addressed to Tom; and in such tone were they rendered that Tom felt he had received full forgiveness.

"Yes, Dick, my friend," answered Tom, gravely. "You can be of great help. Run to the village as fast as you can, and get a wagon or something. We are friends, are we not?"

As Tom spoke, he slipped a silver dollar into Dick's hand. The poor lad with his patched garments, and lacking an overcoat, looked indeed as if he needed the money.

He tried to say something in return for this kindness; but he was unskilled, poor fellow, in the expression of the gentler emotions, and his voice stuck in his throat. He passed a tattered sleeve across his eyes and hurried away.

Even for the expression of gratitude, silence may be golden.

Without further words, Tom and Buck took to the railroad. During their long run, neither spoke. But for all that, every step strengthened between them the friendly feelings so oddly awakened. It was the "touch of nature" —a poor, deserted, dying outcast—that made them kin.

* * * * *

The snow falling almost blindingly. A man lying on the white-robed earth, his face touched and softened by the last prayer for mercy; his features made beautiful by the all-composing hand.

Beside him a kneeling boy absorbed in prayer —heedless of snow and cold, heedless of time and exposure. No words were needed to explain the turn of events to Tom and his rude companion. For one instant they gazed upon the pathetic sight; then, by a common instinct, fell upon their knees beside the dead. And in prayer they all became one.

* ' * * * *

When the wagon arrived, and the dead man had been sheltered under its canvass cover, Buck turned to Percy.

"Do you remember me?" he asked.

Percy looked at him, and, with a sad smile,, nodded his head.

'Would you mind shaking hands ?"

Their hands clasped: they were friends fron? that hour.

CHAPTER XXV

"Farewell, Parting is Such Sweet Sorrow!*'

— Shakespeare

PERCY, when first introduced to the kind reader, was certainly very girlish. As the days of his boarding-school life passed on, some of the more pronounced indications of girlish-ness were rubbed away.

But, in spite of these unboyish ways, his heroism displayed on two occasions, his kindly and sweet disposition, and his unfailing generosity won him the love and respect of his schoolmates. And yet for all that, there was something wanting to round his character. That one thing came with his hour in the cold and the snow beside the dying man. That hour was the hour of crystallization. Percy issued from it a boy—a real boy in every sense of the word. Always kind, cheerful, modest—there came to be added to these sweet traits a certain firmness and manly earnestness. Percy began to look at the world with other, larger eyes. He now saw a world where much good was to be effected, where much evil was to be put down. From that day, then, he looked forward to the doing of some great work. He looked forward with earnestness to the days when as a man he should take a part in the conflict of life, and he was resolved to "be a hero in the strife."

What is this work to be? Time will reveal

it. The work will surely come; for Percy has a fine mind and a noble heart—and why a fine mind and a noble heart, if not for noble deeds ? Whatever this work may be, God, we may be sure, will stamp it with that success which is recognized in its fulness beyond the veil of mortal life.

But a few words more, and, for the present, at least, we are done with our little friends of St. Maure's.

Buck and Dick—we take the heavy villains first—mended from the memorable day of their meeting with Tom and Percy. Slowly, surely, they threw off their rowdyish habits: despite the half-concealed sneers of their old associates, they made heroic and successful attempts towards gaining a higher standard. Their old clothes, like their old manners, were exchanged for better garments. How they contrived to dress so nicely, none of the villagers could explain. However, I am quite certain that Percy Wynn and Tom Playfair could have thrown abundant light upon this mystery. In their improved dress and with their finer manners, both were frequent visitors at the college.

The remaining months ©f the school-year passed on happily. Little Frank, in the course of it, was received into the Church. His temper grows milder with each month, but his sceptical "Prove it, prove it!" is still with him. His success in his studies has been great, and his teacher looks upon his talent for mathematics as something wondrous. Towards Tom and Percy his affection strengthens with each day. He is to spend his vacation with Percy.

wanna t'^u nw^s

Tom is the same little hero — generous, high-minded, gay. In everything he and Percy are as one. He, too, intends to join Percy and Frank for a holiday pleasure-trip. But first he is to spend a few weeks with gentle Aunt Meadow. It is not settled yet whether Harry Quip, Will Ruthers, and Joe Whyte are to be of the party or not. Probably they will; and then hey! for the boating and bathing and fishing on some pretty, retired lake in Wisconsin! I dare say they will have a happy time; for they bear with them, one and all, true heads and sound hearts.

The farewell of Tom and Percy on their homeward route, when they parted at Kansas City— Tom taking the train for St. Louis, and Percy the train for Cincinnati — may be of interest to our readers.

"Good-by, dear old Tom, God bless you! I shall never forget your kindness. YouVe made a boy out of me, sure enough."

"Nonsense!" answered Tom, giving Percy's hand a hearty shake. "Don't talk about boys. You're more than a boy. You're a little man; and you've got there by yourself."

"Well, good-by."

"Good-by—and God bless you!"

We, too, kind readers, repeat Tom's words. "Good-by—and God bless you I"

The End

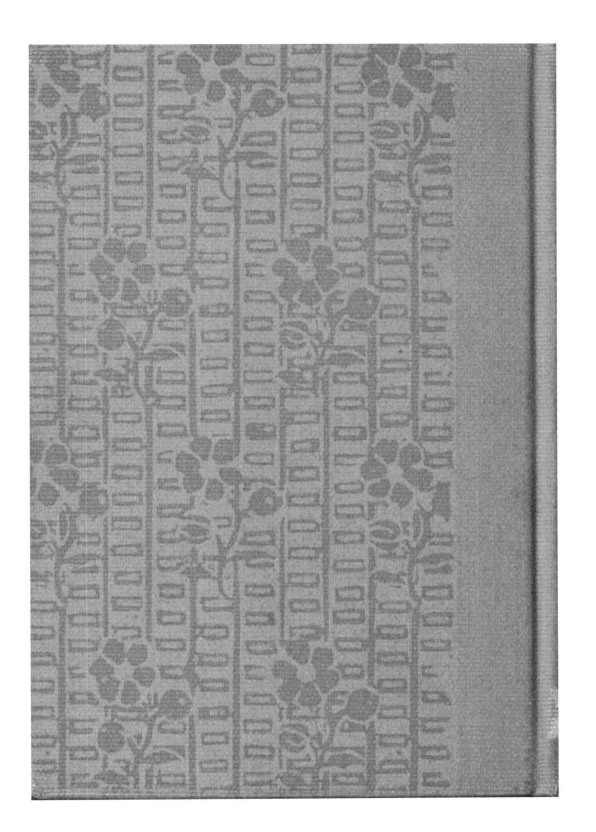

Made in the USA
Las Vegas, NV
16 January 2021